MURDER WITHOUT MOTIVE
THE COMPLETE CASES OF SHOW-
ME McGEE, VOLUME 1

MURDER WITHOUT MOTIVE

THE COMPLETE CASES OF SHOW-ME McGEE, VOLUME 1

FREDERICK C. DAVIS

ILLUSTRATOR
JOSEPH A. FARREN

COVER BY
WALTER DE MARIS

POPULAR PUBLICATIONS · 2024

TABLE OF CONTENTS

HELL ON WHEELS

The Twisted Wreckage of the Automobiles,
and the Grisly Remains of the Men Who
Drove Them, Led Detective McGee
into a Maze of Horror and Mystery

1

JUGGERNAUT

CORNELIUS SELDEN PEERED grimly at the sinister contrivance that lay on his desk—a machine of death. It rested among the loosened wrapping paper that had covered it, a box containing three sticks of dynamite and a device for igniting a short length of fuse. The hands which had built it had planned murder.

Selden's face, firm at sixty, was pale; his gray eyes were fearfully alight. Hours had passed since he had untied the infernal machine; he was still shocked with the realization of how narrowly he had missed death. Somehow the thing had failed to explode.

Some freak of luck had saved Selden from horrible destruction.

He gazed again at the scrawled writing on the wrapping paper. It was laboriously disguised: his own name was there as the addressee, and above it were printed the words, *Strictly Personal.* There was another name, apparently that of the sender:

From: A. Zorda,

              30 Eternity St.,

              City.

Cornelius Selden strode across the spacious library and back, his dressing-gown flapping around his long legs. He paused and glanced at the clock on the fireplace mantel: fifty minutes until midnight. He grabbed the phone.

"Police Headquarters!"

The big house was silent. In it only one light was burning: the lamp on the desk, which centered its rays on the diabolical machine of death. Waiting, Cornelius Selden peered at it, and shuddered.

There was a gigantic explosion
and a splash of flame as some
terrible thing struck the car

"Police Headquarters?" he asked as the connection was made. "I want to speak to the Chief of Detectives. Cornelius Selden calling. It's very important."

The line clicked; a new voice came through.

"Lieutenant Detective McGee talking."

"Oh, yes, Mr. McGee; I've heard of you," Selden said quickly. "I want you to come to my home immediately. There has been an attempt to kill me."

"Kill you?"

Selden paused, listening. A sound came into the library through the closed windows: a steady, smooth drone. It was the exhaust noise of an airplane passing overhead. It grew louder, suddenly, as Selden spoke again into the transmitter.

"Yes. Late this afternoon I received an infernal machine

Yellow fumes came drifting
back on the wind

through the mail. I've hesitated to call you because I want to avoid newspaper publicity if possible. If you'll—"

Selden broke off abruptly. The drone of the passing airplane had turned into a loud snarl: but it was not that sound which startled him. It was another noise, sharp and sudden and close at hand. A quick crashing of glass!

Selden twisted swiftly, in time to see a pane of the French door burst as something broke through. It thumped to the rug—something heavy and black. It rolled and stopped while Selden stared. It lay within a few feet of him: it was sputtering and fuming, and sparks were flying from it!

Selden uttered a terrified ejaculation, and recoiled. The phone slipped from his fingers, clattered to the floor. One instant he stared at the thing near his feet—the hissing, smoking object. He made a quick move toward it; he stopped in horror; suddenly he rushed across the room toward the French door.

He clicked the latch swiftly and darted through. As he sprang into the darkness he called frantically, "Fletch! Fletch!" The next instant the earth seemed to burst asunder with fiery violence, and Cornelius Selden felt himself flung forward with terrific power.

A report like a thunderbolt shook the house, shocked through the ground, jolted the air. Leaping flame burst through the shattered windows of the library. Fragments of glass flew like shrapnel. Flung to the ground, Selden could see nothing of what happened behind him; the shock of the explosion stunned him.

It was over in an instant. Selden pulled himself up, gasping for breath, peering back. The light inside the library had gone out, but the glow of the moon showed him the destruction that had been wrought. Every window of the library had burst; yellowish-white fumes were pouring out.

Selden ran impulsively to the broken French door, choking in the stinging air. Inside he could see, dimly, chaotic destruction fogged by the thick fumes. Furniture had been hurled aside, broken. Sections of the walls showed bare laths; the floor was littered with broken plaster, and in the center of the room was a gaping hole. Selden backed away, gasping again:

"Fletcher! Fletcher!"

At a window of the floor above, a pale, strained face appeared. Cornelius Selden heard movements upstairs, quick footfalls on the steps. In a moment a dark figure came groping through the French door of an adjoining room. A youngish man hurried to Cornelius Selden's side. "Dad! Good Lord! What happened?"

"Fletcher! Are you all right?"

"Yes—sure. I was thrown out of bed, but are you hurt, Dad?"

"No—no, I'm all right, Fletch! Good Heaven, I—" Cornelius Selden broke off, staring in horror at his older son. "It was a bomb!"

He hurried toward the broken French door again, and groped his way into the demolished room. The air was still thick with acrid fumes; the break in the floor had weakened it dangerously; but Cornelius Selden found his way to the telephone. He picked it up, rattled the hook.

"Hello!" he called. "Hello! Headquarters!"

There was no answer. The line was dead....

A BROAD STONE gateway gave entrance to the expansive estate of Cornelius Selden. A pair of headlights flashed through it as a car swung off the road and spurted along the driveway toward the house. It creaked to a sudden stop; a big man wedged himself away from the wheel as a smaller one jumped out the opposite door. They hurried across the lawn toward the gleam of candlelight issuing through the library windows.

The big man led the way. He paused, peering about: his gaze stopped on Cornelius Selden, who was standing just inside the French door. He sniffed the air and said:

"Dynamite! Some mess!"

The candlelight shone upon utter wreckage. Nothing in the room was unharmed. A fine tapestry hanging on one wall was tattered; several oil portraits were ripped; the mantel was torn off the fireplace. "I'm McGee, from Head-quarters," the big man said briskly. "You were talking to me when this happened. I came beating it out here right away. The gent with me is Detective Sergeant Baxter. Anybody hurt?"

Cornelius Selden was still breathless. "No—fortunately! As I was talking to you, Mr. McGee, a bomb was thrown through the window. I ran out of the room just before it exploded. If I'd been a second slower—it would have killed me!"

"Me, I don't believe much," said McGee laconically, "but I believe that, all right. A bomb, you said? Then, it wasn't the infernal machine that exploded?"

"No. The machine was on my desk—harmless," Corne-lius Selden explained quickly. "It—it's there."

McGee followed Cornelius Selden's pointing finger to the corner. A box was lying there, wrapping paper still clinging to it.

McGee picked it up, brought it near a candle, and eyed it.

"Didn't explode even when the bomb went off. Guess the desk must've shielded it. That's lucky—now we've got something to trace." He straightened, peering at the shocked old man. "You got any idea who did this, Mr. Selden? Any idea who's trying to kill you?"

"No—none whatever!" Cornelius Selden exclaimed.

"You must've beat it outside right on the heels of the guy who tossed the bomb through the window. Did you see him?" McGee asked.

"I—I scarcely had time to see anything," the old man answered breathlessly. "I was still running out of the door when the bomb exploded. No—I didn't see the man who threw it in."

"Whoever he was," observed McGee wryly, "he's trying hard as hell to kill you, Mr. Selden. First an infernal machine, then a bomb. He must've tossed in the bomb to do the job the machine failed to do. That's an ugly way to try to kill a man, I'll say!"

McGee bent over the wrappings, deciphered the sender's name, and straightened.

" 'A. Zorda.' There's no such place as Eternity Street in this town that I know of. Know anybody by the name of Zorda?"

"I never heard the name before!"

McGee turned, thrust the infernal machine into Baxter's hands.

"Box-Car, take this thing down to Headquarters and get rid of the dynamite. Check up on the name and address. I guess I'd better stick around here a while." Turning back to Cornelius Selden, he asked: "Is it possible this thing wasn't thrown at you by some one on the ground? Over the telephone I heard an airplane just before the explosion."

"I doubt if the plane had anything to do with it," Selden answered quickly. "I saw the bomb come through the window. It couldn't possibly have been thrown through the window by anyone in a plane."

"Guess that's right," McGee observed reluctantly, "except maybe it was an autogyro. Then—well, hell! I don't believe in cooking up fancy theories. You can't trust much of anything, let alone theories."

He took a turn about the damaged room, glancing now and again at Cornelius and Fletcher Selden. He knew these two gentlemen by sight; that was a detective's business. They were one of the wealthiest families in the city, socially prominent, respected. And at the moment they were exceedingly upset.

"Somebody meant business, all right!" McGee observed. "If you don't mind, I'll stick here all night and take a look around. I don't expect to find any clews to the dynamiter, but I've got to look. You'd better try to get some rest."

"Yes," said Cornelius Selden. "Of course."

As McGee moved out the French doors, he heard the sound of another car purring through the gateway. The headlights swept across the lawn, swung around the police sedan, and stopped by the large garage at the rear.

"Go on, beat it to Headquarters, Box-Car," McGee said glumly. "Take the car, and come back early in the morning to relieve me. Somebody better be watching Selden continually from now on. When somebody tries as hard as this to kill a man, he won't give up."

"You mean the dynamiter threw the bomb because the infernal machine didn't work, and because the bomb didn't get Selden he'll take another crack at the old man?" Baxter asked.

"It's an idea, Box-Car," McGee answered. "You know I'm kind of skeptical about ideas, but we've got to play safe. Now beat it."

A young man was hurrying from the car which had stopped near the garage. He brought up short, eying McGee and Baxter—a young, handsome chap. Alarmed, he stepped through the door, peered around the wrecked room, and blurted:

"Great Scott, Dad, what happened?"

Cornelius Selden mopped his forehead nervously. "Mr. McGee," he introduced, "this is my younger son, Bradford. Mr. McGee is a detective, Brad."

Brad Selden shook hands with McGee briefly. Again he stared around the room and again he blurted:

"What happened?"

"Somebody," said McGee as he stepped out the door again, "seems to have shot off a firecracker."

SHOW-ME McGEE WAS eating an excellent breakfast in the kitchen of the Selden home when he heard the sound of a car on the driveway and looked out to see Baxter braking the police sedan to a stop. Gesturing with a piece of toast, he went on talking with the chubby Irish cook.

"My old man, Mrs. Murphy," he said, "was a cop, like me, and a damn' good one. He used to tell me, 'Son,' he used to say, 'keep your head. In this world you can believe only about a tenth of what you read, a quarter of what you hear, and half of what you see.' I live by his teaching, Mrs.

Murphy. Now you, for instance. You don't look much like a cook, but you can make swell coffee."

"Have another cup," said Mrs. Murphy, very pleased.

McGee was stirring it when Baxter came in the door. Baxter took a chair and sighed.

"Nothing doing, Show-Me," he reported. "There's nobody in town by the name of A. Zorda that I can find, and there isn't any such street as Eternity."

"Sure not," said McGee, raising his cup. "No more than there're any clews around this place. Not a clew to show who did it. But," he added, "even if I'd found a hundred of 'em, I wouldn't believe 'em."

"Didn't you find out anything, Show-Me?" Baxter asked.

McGee took a swallow of coffee. "Fletcher, the oldest son, was upstairs asleep when it happened. Brad, the younger one, was seeing his girl last night. It was the servants' night off. The old man hasn't an idea in the world who would want to kill him. Add that up and what do you get? Zero!"

McGee's eyes lifted as Cornelius Selden appeared in the dining-room doorway. His face was drawn; he looked weary. Now he was trimly dressed in a business suit, and he was carrying a brief-case.

"I am going to the bank, Mr. McGee," he announced. "Can I drive you to town?"

"No, thanks, I'm taking the police-car," McGee answered. "Baxter is going to stick around and keep an eye on you. We'll follow you into town, and Baxter will keep you company—just to make sure nothing else happens."

"I—I'm completely at sea!" Selden exclaimed. "Thank

you for your trouble, Mr. McGee. I want to leave immediately—can you?"

McGee rose, draining his cup, and nodded. Cornelius
Selden, walking with dignified stride, stepped out the
kitchen door. McGee and Baxter followed him along the
driveway. As Selden threw open the doors of the garage,
the two detectives piled into the police sedan.

Selden backed out a heavy, twelve-cylinder coupé and
sent it rolling toward the gate. McGee, starting his motor,
followed. He swung the police car after Selden's, and kept
his distance as the coupé began rolling toward the city.

The road led through five miles of open country, and
spaced along it sat wealthy estates. Selden drove at a
moderate speed, and McGee kept pace. Settling back, he
sighed.

"Guys don't commit murder for the fun of it," he
commented dryly. "There's got to be something in it. In
Selden's case it looks like money would be a good reason for
killing him—he's got a mountain of it. What a place he's
got! Only, who'd get the money if old Selden was bumped
off? Only his two sons, Fletcher and Brad."

"Thinking of them, Show-Me?" Baxter asked.

"Thinking—that's all. Not drawing any conclusions,"
McGee answered. "Now, an ordinary cop would say, 'Why,
sure, one of the two sons is trying to kill the old man for
his money.' Me, I don't believe it. It'd be the most natural
thing in the world to suspect 'em, so it can't be trusted."

McGee frowned, sat forward, peered out the window
as though looking for something, and settled back again.

"Then we've got to find out who else would profit by the
old guy's death," Baxter suggested.

"Nobody else but the two sons," McGee answered. "I asked questions about that right away. Nobody but— what's that, anyway?"

McGee put his head out the window of the car and glanced upward. A droning noise came out of the sky, and he soon found its source—an airplane. He squinted at it and determined it wasn't an ordinary airplane after all. It was an autogyro, hovering high over the road, its grotesque vanes revolving slowly.

"That's funny," McGee observed with a frown. "An airplane passed over Selden's place just before the explosion last night and now there's another one right above—"

The words were blasted back down his throat.

Without warning a terrific concussion shook the air. McGee jerked his head in swiftly, peered ahead. A flash of blazing fire spewed out of the road a hundred yards away, directly at the spot Cornelius Selden's coupé was passing!

One instant the car ahead was enveloped in the thundering flame! The next instant the fire was gone, and the coupé was careening through a mass of gusting smoke! It lurched to the side of the road swiftly, half in the air; it fell with a terrifying crash into the ditch. There it lay, a fuming, misshapen wreck!

2

SUSPECTED AND DEAD

SHOW-ME McGEE THREW his two hundred pounds desperately against the brake pedal. The windshield in front of his eyes cracked, turned starry white, as a flying bit of metal struck it. He swung to the side of the road, lurched back with the emergency, jammed himself out the car door. He stood in the road a moment, staring at the remains of Selden's coupé, appalled.

"God, he got it that time!" Baxter gasped.

McGee ran forward heavily, his face grim and hard. Suddenly he stopped, peering again into the air. The autogyro was still directly overhead, above the road, its motor droning and its vanes spinning. McGee jerked at his hip-pocket holster, swung out his automatic, but held it without raising it.

"Looks like that thing dropped another bomb on Selden!" Baxter blurted.

The plane's registration number, painted on its wing, was photographed on McGee's mind. It was out of range of his gun; he was temperamentally doubtful of a connection between the autogyro and the demolished coupé. Suddenly he spurted forward again, trotted along the road to the wreck.

He swung open the door, reached inside, but instantly withdrew. His face pictured nausea and horror. He slammed the door shut again and faced Baxter.

Baxter was peering up. "That thing's coming down!" he exclaimed.

McGee's eyes followed Baxter's, and he verified the fact. The autogyro was dropping almost vertically, evidently maneuvering toward an open field at the side of the road. McGee's big hand closed over Baxter's arm.

"Don't look in if you want to keep your breakfast," he warned grimly. "God, it's horrible! Selden got it all right— he's in pieces. Stay here—keep other cars away if they stop!"

He shot a glance up again, at the plane. It was dropping more rapidly now. McGee held his gun ready and began to trot in the direction of its selected landing place. He reached a stone wall and clambered over it. He ran again, puffing, as the gyro dropped low.

Its trucks struck the earth; it bounced slightly, slid along. A helmeted, leather-jacketed pilot raised from the pit, dropped over the side. McGee brought himself to a quick stop, gulping in air.

The pilot of the gyro was Brad Selden!

THE YOUNGER SON of the dead man hurried anxiously toward McGee.

"That was Dad's car, wasn't it? What's happened? Is he hurt?"

McGee answered stiffly: "I guess you know it was your Dad's car, all right. He's more than hurt. You take my advice and stay away from there, understand?"

"Is he—"

"He's dead."

McGee watched the expression of horror and pain come over Brad Selden's face. The young man was stunned, strengthless for the moment. McGee roughly took his arm, turned him about, led him back to the gyro.

"Stay here!" he ordered.

"But if—if—"

"Stay here!"

McGee cast a grim eye upon the gyro. He crouched, peered at its underside. He straightened, thrust his head into the pit. He spent a swift moment inspecting the dials and controls, then backed away. Again he surveyed young Selden grimly.

"Damn' nasty," he said. "Especially when it looks a hell of a lot like you dropped a bomb on that car!"

"I dropped—!" Brad Selden broke off, speechless.

"How'd it happen you were right above the car when it exploded? Last night there was a plane above the house just before the bomb went off, and this morning you were right above that car when it blew up. It looks damn' funny!"

Brad Selden swallowed hard before he answered. "I often—often dropped down and signalled Dad on his way to town. I—" Suddenly anger seized him. "McGee, are you insinuating—? Dad was the finest man in the world. If you think—"

"I'm not thinking—I'm just watching," McGee interrupted stonily. "Suppose it happened to be you that flew over the house last night just before—"

"I—I've often done that, too. I didn't know anything'd happened there—I tell you I—" Again he broke off, overcome. "The field isn't far from the house, and Dad always knew when he heard the plane that I'd be home in about half an hour. I—"

"You *were* in the plane last night, then!" McGee blurted. "I'll be damned! You didn't say so before! All I found out from you—"

"I told you I was with Miss Holland last night, and I was! She was with me in the gyro… McGee, for God's sake—"

"Take it easy," McGee warned. "You own a commercial field west of your home, don't you? You were heading for it last night, about the time the bomb wrecked the library? Young guy, this looks bad, but I'm reserving my opinion, and you and I are heading for the field right now."

"I've got to go over there!" Brad Selden exclaimed. "I've got to see Dad. You can't expect me—"

"I expect you to do as I say!" McGee snapped. "Resisting an officer isn't healthy, fella. Stay here—get in that plane. I'm going with you to your field, understand? I'll be back in a second."

McGee left Brad Selden standing stunned beside the gyro. He hurried to the stone wall, legged over it, trotted along the road, and shouted to Baxter.

"Stay on the job, Box-Car! I'm flying back and phoning Nelson." Nelson was the Medical Examiner. "The quicker we get old Selden out of there, the better. Keep everybody away and beat it back to the house as soon as you can!"

McGee hurried over the wall again, toward the gyro. Brad Selden was automatically getting into the pit. McGee heaved his hulk over the cowling, wedged himself into the seat beside young Selden, and signalled him to take off.

He held his hat as the engine roared and the vanes

circled. The machine took a short run and lifted. Brad Selden, pale and shocked, manipulated the controls automatically, sending the machine into a climb. McGee watched the ground drop away swiftly and held on.

"I don't trust these things," he muttered.

Brad Selden did not speak as he sent the gyro across the sky. Looking down, McGee saw the road pass, the wrecked car and Baxter guarding it. Soon they were sweeping over the expansive grounds of the Selden estate, toward a square, flat field beyond.

McGee surveyed the neat layout of the airport as the gyro swung above it and began to settle. Along one side was a row of trim hangars, and beside it a small shack; a white picket fence enclosed the field. The tiny figure of a man hurried from the shack and onto the field as the gyro swung in for a landing.

A bounce, a skip, and the machine was down. McGee legged out. Brad Selden followed dazedly. McGee looked about, judged he would find a telephone in the office shack, and strode toward it. Inside he found desks, chairs, cabinets and neatness. He grasped up the phone and asked for Headquarters.

"Sullivan," he said as the connection came through. "McGee. Sully, we've got a murder—a big one. Cornelius Selden blown to hell and gone. 'Blown' is what I said. Get Doc Nelson out on the Pike Road as fast as he can move— Baxter's on the spot. And keep it out of the newspapers."

McGee left the office shack and trudged back to the gyro. Brad Selden had been talking with the other man; they grew silent as McGee peered at the plane. Awkwardly, stooping under it and climbing over it, he made an inspection. As he drew back, Brad Selden's companion stepped up to him.

"Can I help you?"

"Not unless you can show me some kind of a bomb-release dingus on that contraption!" McGee snapped.

"I'm afraid you'll find nothing of that sort on the plane," the other answered. "My name is Lambert, Mr. McGee—Edgar Lambert. I'm a friend of the Seldens. I've just heard of the terrible thing that happened. I hardly know what to say, but if there is anything I can do to help—"

"Thanks; maybe there is," McGee answered. "Lambert? I've heard of you. You've got an airplane factory near here, haven't you?"

"Yes; I'm an aeronautical engineer, and my plant is on this road. Brad has a fleet of my planes here. If—"

McGee stepped toward Brad Selden. "I don't want to be hard on you," he said. "It looks a lot like you bombed that car, but that's why I don't believe it—I'll admit it. I'm skeptical of appearances, but at the same time I'm skeptical of my own reactions. I want to take a look around here."

"Certainly," young Selden said. He turned to Lambert. "Show McGee around, will you, Ed? I—I'm a bit shaken up. I—"

"I want to know," said McGee, "if you've got any explosives around here."

"No; certainly not."

"Well, I'm from Missouri, and that isn't any figure of speech, either," McGee retorted. "Go ahead—take it easy, Selden."

Brad Selden walked toward the office shack in a stupor. McGee surveyed the line of hangars and began to trudge toward them. He was halfway there when he heard a *put-putting* on the road that ran behind the sheds. Abruptly he broke into a run and stopped at the picket fence.

A motorcycle officer was whizzing in his direction. McGee waved his arms in signal. The officer brought his machine to a stop.

"Taggert," said McGee, "stick around. Stay right there by the gate, will you? I want you to keep an eye on this place."

"Okay, Show-Me," said Taggert.

McGee trudged back to the hangars. Lambert followed him, and threw open the big doors for him. McGee found three big planes in their places, like nesting birds with spread wings. Lambert cabin-jobs, all of them. He walked around the planes, looking into odd places.

Lambert said nothing as McGee made his search. He peered behind oil barrels, into lockers, in the drawers of the tool-bench—everywhere he could think of. In the second hangar he repeated the process. Now and again he glanced at his watch—the fat timepiece bequeathed him by his father, old Dan McGee, bless his soul… At last, when he finished the search, McGee looked despondent.

"Well, I didn't expect to find anything," he observed. "I want to go over to the Selden place."

"I'll drive you," Lambert offered promptly. "Perhaps it would be better to let Brad stay here until he recovers from the shock."

McGee nodded, trudged out of the hangar. He walked to the gate, where Taggert was waiting with his machine, and said: "Watch young Selden, Tag. He's not to go up in any more airplanes—that's orders. Understand?"

Taggert understood. Lambert was walking toward a

sedan parked near the gate; McGee followed him. In a moment the machine was swinging out of the gate with Lambert at the wheel, McGee slumped beside him. For half a mile they rode in silence.

"This is serious business, McGee," Lambert observed. "A mistake would be tragic."

"You mean you don't think Brad Selden did it?"

"Of course he didn't. He told me of what you'd said to him, you know. Suppose we look at it from an impersonal angle. You seem to believe that someone in a plane tossed a bomb through the window of the Selden place last night, and that Brad's plane dropped a bomb on Cornelius Selden's car a little while ago. It's no good as a theory, McGee."

"Why not?" McGee answered.

"Too accurate shooting. Remember, a plane is a moving vehicle. To think that a man in a gyro could hit a window with a bomb, then hit a car with another bomb—register two straight hits—it's too much. It's perfection. One hundred per cent bull's-eyes. It couldn't be done."

"Theories are no good anyway," McGee said glumly.

The car was whizzing along the tar road in the direction of the Selden estate.

"To go on," Lambert said. "Dynamite was used last night, Brad said. Dropping dynamite from a plane onto a car would present no end of problems. First, the aim, but let that go. Suppose the fuse were too short—it would explode in the air before it hit the car. Suppose it were too long—it probably would hit the top of the car, but the impact might not be enough to explode it. In that case it would roll off, and the car would be far ahead by the time the explosion came.

"To register a perfect shot would mean gauging the altitude of the plane to a hair, the length of the fuse to a fraction of an inch. There's too many factors involved, McGee. It's just not possible. And to assume some other kind of bomb was used—some percussion bomb—that's too much, too. They can't be had, and nobody could make one but a skilled workman."

"In other words," McGee answered, "it couldn't've been done. Maybe not. But old Selden was certainly blown to pieces."

"Yes," said Lambert, "but you'll have to look farther than Brad Selden for the murderer, McGee. Brad is one of the finest young chaps who ever lived."

McGee was silent. The sedan turned abruptly, and swung into the driveway of the Selden estate. McGee saw the police sedan parked near the garage, and knew that Baxter had returned. As he approached the house, McGee hurried ahead of Lambert and met Baxter coming out of the kitchen door.

"Doc Nelson took old Selden into town, Show-Me," Baxter said. "Fletcher Selden is here. What the hell'll we do now?"

McGee asked in a whisper: "Phone fixed?"

"Yes."

"Beat it in and phone Sullivan," McGee said. "Make sure nobody hears you do it. Ask Sullivan to get a quick financial report on Fletcher Selden—credit rating. It won't take a minute—bring it back with you."

Baxter hurried in through the kitchen door. McGee

went around to the entrance of the wrecked library. It was a hopeless shambles. He was staring in when Fletcher Selden came from the front of the house.

The elder son of the murdered man looked wan, distraught. He was silent, unable to find words to address McGee.

"I'm sorry as hell," McGee said solemnly, "but there was no way of stopping it. There's no use of my saying anything. But if you don't mind, I've got to ask some dumb questions."

"Yes—certainly."

"Don't you usually drive into town with your father in the morning?"

"Yes; I usually do," Fletcher answered nervously. "This morning I had to wait. I had an appointment with a client here this morning; I've just finished with him."

McGee nodded; he knew that the elder Selden had been a banker, that Fletcher was a broker. "Brad and his father," he asked slowly, "were on good terms, I suppose?"

"The best. Brad admired and loved Dad. We are— were—uncommonly happy together, the three of us. Brad is true blue—proud, independent, sincere—"

"Operating an airport mustn't be so profitable these days," McGee observed.

"It isn't. Brad has had and is having a tough time. In fact, he is all but bankrupt."

"Ah?" said McGee.

"But that—that couldn't possibly—" Fletcher checked his impulsive protest. "Brad started the airport with an inheritance received from our grandfather. He sank all his money in the field. Dad and I offered to help him out—

lend him, or give him what money he needs—but he refused. That's Brad. He wants to make good on his own, without help from anyone else."

Fletcher Selden's voice lowered. "I know what you must be thinking, McGee. No one can profit through Dad's death but Brad and I. I can't blame you for thinking that— but there's nothing in it. I tell you sincerely that I have more money of my own than I know what to do with. And there would scarcely be reason for Brad's killing his father—hideous as that thought is—to get money, when he might have had all he needed by simply saying he'd take it."

"He could've had every penny he needed?" McGee asked slowly. "Just by asking for it?"

"Every last cent, as simply as that," Fletcher Selden declared.

"It certainly goes to show that you can't trust any theories worth a damn!" McGee sighed. "You going to town now? If you are, Baxter and I will follow you along. I've got to get to Headquarters—feel this thing out."

"Certainly," Selden said.

McGee walked to the police car as Fletcher Selden strode to the garage. McGee could see two other cars in their places in the large structure. Baxter hurried from the kitchen, and kept silent at McGee's signal as they piled into their sedan.

Fletcher Selden backed around, started for the gate. McGee followed slowly in the police car, gesturing a farewell to Lambert, who was returning to his own automobile. Once out the gate, Selden's car accelerated; McGee followed it easily.

"Well?" he asked Baxter.

"Sullivan got the dope for me while I waited—just a credit report. Fletcher's all right. Plenty of money behind him. That lead's no good, Show-Me."

"Neither is any other, Box-Car," said McGee morosely. "So far it doesn't make sense. A gullible cop, now—he'd be throwing Fletcher and Brad into the jug *toot sweet*. You can't trust the first idea that pops into your head, though. You can't trust anything. Look at the Kellogg Peace Pact, and there's Japan—"

He broke off abruptly, uttering an exclamation. Through the air he sensed a loud humming sound. Abruptly he poked his head out the window and peered into the sky.

"Hey!" he exclaimed.

Above them an autogyro was maneuvering! McGee glimpsed the number on its wing—the same number he had seen earlier that morning! The same ship! There it was now, almost directly above the road, and swinging closer!

"I hear it!" Baxter gasped. "Gosh, Show-Me, we're almost at the spot where—"

Thunder-clap!

The terrific blast of sound came without warning! In the road almost a hundred yards ahead appeared a gigantic splash of flame!

In an instant it completely blotted out the car that Fletcher Selden was driving!

McGee jerked back to the wheel, desperately swift. The force of the explosion and the shock to his nerves sent the police car swerving to the side of the road. Yellow fumes came ripping back on the wind as McGee yelled hoarsely and jammed on the brakes.

Instantaneously the car ahead was seized in the grip of

a terrible power. Its top flaming, it lurched toward the side of the road, lifted from the ground. As it struck, one of its wheels tore off. It lurched into the gully with a rending crash, and there it rested—wrecked as the car of Cornelius Selden had been wrecked!

3

MCGEE TAKES IT

McGEE RECKLESSLY SWUNG the police sedan to the side of the road, slammed it to a stop, hopped out. Baxter hastened after him as they sprinted toward the ruin of Fletcher Selden's car.

An area of the road was still fuming, blasted open by the force of the explosion.

McGee stared through the broken car window, backed away and uttered "God!" The interior of the car was afire. Hastily he dropped into the ditch, grasped up handfuls of loose earth, and flung them at the flames. Baxter helped him, working feverishly. Five minutes of fast work put the fire out.

Thick smoke poured out of the twisted body of the car as McGee peered upward into the sky, as Baxter pointed along the road, horrified. "Look, Show-Me! The old man's car is right ahead!"

McGee wasn't looking at things like that. He peered into the interior of the car again, then back into the sky.

"Blown to bits!" he exclaimed breathlessly. "God, what a horrible death! Listen, Box-Car! Stick here—I've got my eye on that machine up there!"

"Lord—two in the same morning, in the same way!" Baxter gulped.

Still staring up, McGee began moving back toward the police sedan. His eyes were on the hovering autogyro. This time it was sailing away—it wasn't coming down. McGee clambered into the sedan, swung swiftly about on the road, poked his head out the window, and saw the gyro swinging west.

He slammed the car into high and began speeding along the road in the direction of the Selden estate. Continually he peered out the window, glancing upward, keeping the gyro in sight. It was still droning west, and it appeared to be dropping. When trees blotted it from sight, McGee raced ahead until the clear sky opened above him again.

He sped past the Selden place while the gyro was circling far out. Swiftly McGee swung a turn at an intersection, again picked up speed. He kept the accelerator clamped down, his gaze on the strange craft in the air. It was beginning to circle back now, at a lazy rate.

Miles flashed past McGee as he grimly kept his speedometer flickering at the seventy mark and watched the revolving vanes in the sky....

Ahead, suddenly, he saw the picket fence and the neat layout of the airport. At the same time he saw the autogyro sinking, swinging toward the field. With a chuckle of triumph, McGee wheezed more speed out of his motor. "Nobody'll be able to ditch anything out of that plane before I get to it!" he told himself.

The gyro was sliding downward toward the tarmac as McGee slid to a smoking stop near the gate of the field.

Hopping out, he saw Officer Taggert still on duty just inside. He strode toward Taggert, eyes blazing.

"Tag, I told you not to let Selden go back up! What the devil do you mean letting Selden go—"

"Selden? That wasn't Selden who went up, was it? It didn't look like him to me."

"Yah! A cop's got no business taking anything for granted!" McGee stormed.

Now the gyro was settling. Its trucks struck the ground, and it rolled along a few yards as McGee legged heavily toward it. He glanced aside once to see Edgar Lambert hurrying toward him; Lambert had returned to the field from the Selden place. Close to the plane, McGee stopped.

The pilot, back turned, was getting out. McGee stepped forward, opened his mouth, and was about to speak when the pilot turned. McGee did not speak; surprise stifled his words.

He was looking into the face of a very pretty girl!

McGee glanced around dazedly. He saw Lambert behind him; and, farther away, he saw Brad Selden coming from the office shack. McGee looked again at the leather-uniformed young lady and sighed.

She was worried, anxious. She glanced at McGee, hurried past him toward Lambert. Stopping, speaking in a hushed tone, she said:

"Ed—I saw something terrible on the road—another explosion. Don't let Brad hear. It was like—"

McGee interrupted her. "You saw it, did you? Well, it happens that I saw you directly above the road when that car exploded. This is no time to spare anybody's feelings.

Fletcher Selden was in that car—and the explosion killed him!"

The girl whirled to face McGee; she grew deathly pale. Brad Selden, hearing McGee's words, stopped short and stared mutely. Lambert looked about confusedly, speechless. McGee surveyed them all, grimly, angrily.

"Twice now cars've been blown to hell and gone with a plane directly above 'em! The first time it looked queer enough, and now—" McGee expelled his breath violently. "Young woman, I don't know who you are, but you've got a hell of a lot of explaining to do before I—"

"McGee," Lambert interrupted quietly, "this young lady is Miss Diane Holland—Brad's fiancée."

"Holland?" McGee barked. "Diane Holland?"

His shoulders sagged heavily. He had never before set eyes upon Miss Diane Holland, but he knew her name well. It appeared frequently in the society columns of the newspapers. The Holland name belonged to one of the finest families of the region—a family even wealthier, even more highly respected than the Seldens!

A young lady of Diane Holland's enviable standing, McGee realized instantly, could not conceivably be associated with murder.

IT WAS LATE afternoon when McGee made ready to leave the airport. He had spent disheartening hours trying to find a thread to follow, something that might possibly lead him to the secret of the two Selden deaths. His every effort had been futile.

He had questioned Miss Holland at length. She was distressed and upset, but she had told a coherent story. She was a licensed pilot and had come to Brad's field for her daily flight. Only chance had brought her above the Pike Road. She had not seen the explosion, but had felt its force, had lingered in the air almost afraid to land and tell what she had seen because of the possible effect it might have on Brad. She knew nothing of the explosion: nothing.

McGee had inspected the autogyro: the same machine Brad had flown earlier in the morning. There was absolutely no suspicious detail about it. He had searched the field and the hangars again, without result. There was nothing hidden, nothing sinister, in the layout of the airport.

Disgusted and weary, McGee left Diane Holland with Brad Selden, and piled into the police sedan. Edgar Lambert followed him and asked seriously:

"McGee, frankly, do you believe that Brad is mixed up in this?"

"I don't believe anything," McGee answered. "I don't even believe that I don't believe anything. I don't know. It's got me dizzy."

"You must be off on the wrong track, McGee. It simply isn't possible that both cars were bombed from the air. It's impossible to imagine—"

"It's impossible, but it happened—uh-huh," answered McGee. "I know what you're driving at. Brad's a friend of yours, and you don't want trouble for him. I don't believe he did it, no—at the same time I don't believe he didn't do it—and no matter what I believe, there's something else to be considered. The law."

"You mean you may arrest him—in spite of all—"

"What I mean is," said McGee wearily, "I'm dizzy!"

He started the car, swung into the gate, and stopped.

Officer Taggert was still there, perched on the seat of his motorcycle. McGee sighed at him:

"Get somebody from Headquarters to relieve you, Tag—and tell 'em that no plane is to leave this field until I say the word, no matter who's in it—understand?"

"Okay."

McGee turned onto the road and sped away. With the Selden home his destination, he followed the highway. Twenty minutes later he rolled through the gate and stopped beside the garage. He walked into the kitchen and found Mrs. Murphy drawing something flat and brown from the oven.

"Just look at that, Mr. McGee," said the cook. "It's terrible! It fell, and the flavor's no good. That cake is just waste, but the magazine said it was one of the best cake recipes ever."

"Mrs. Murphy," McGee sighed, sinking into a chair, "you can't trust anything."

IT WAS DARK, and McGee was pacing back and forth across the living room, when he heard a car draw onto the grounds. He was still pacing back and forth when Baxter came in from the direction of the kitchen.

"This," said Baxter, "is a hell of a mess."

"It's worse than that, Box-Car," McGee snapped. "Two bloody murders in one morning is worse than a mess. The Chief'll put me back on the gas-house beat if I don't get somewhere on this. Go on out and talk with Mrs. Murphy—I'm thinking."

Baxter shrugged and left. McGee kept walking back and forth. Minutes later he heard another car roll along the driveway, but he paid little attention to it… Suddenly,

eyes brightened with an idea, he stepped toward the telephone, picked it up, and called Headquarters.

"Sullivan," he said. "I want another credit-rating—and
this time I want everything you can get. It's important. I
want you to get the dope on—"

An opening door interrupted him. Looking around, he
saw Brad Selden entering. Diane Holland was with him,
her flying suit changed for a smart, bright dress.

"Never mind, Sully! I'll call you later," McGee said into
the phone, and abandoned it.

He took a deep breath and spoke to Brad Selden.

"M'boy, I've been thinking all this over. Thinking it over
from all angles, asking myself who, and why, and how, and
what, and all the rest of it. And I've come to the conclusion
that there's only one thing to do—take you to Headquarters and hold you."

Brad Selden's eyes sharpened; Diane caught her breath;
but they said nothing.

"I'm a cop, and I hope I'm a good one," McGee went on,
"but I'm no grand jury and I'm no judge. I shouldn't try to
be. It's my business to find facts and turn 'em over to the
judiciary. I'm not arresting you, understand—but you've
got to talk to the District Attorney."

"Yes," Brad Selden said slowly; "I suppose so."

"What the District Attorney does will be his own business," McGee went on. "He'll question you. He may order
you held without bail for the grand jury. If he does that, and
the grand jury indicts you, it'll mean you'll go to trial for
murder. The evidence is mighty slim, but there's no telling
what can happen—the D.A.'s a tough bird—but there's
nothing else I can do."

Diane Holland exclaimed: "But it's absurd to think—"

"I don't think anything, Miss Holland," McGee interrupted. "Either for or against that young man—I don't
think anything. I'd feel better if I did. But I guess he'd
better come along."

"Very well," said Brad Selden. "I'll go whenever you say."

"Right now," McGee pronounced. "Come along."

"Brad!"

Diane grasped Brad's hands; suddenly he enclosed her
in his arms. McGee looked, blinked, and waited. Brad
Selden took the girl's arms from him, turned grimly, and
marched toward McGee at the door. He passed through
without a word.

McGee glanced at the girl, saw her eyes were full of
tears, and hastily withdrew. Brad Selden was walking across
the lawn to the garage; McGee followed him. Near the
police sedan the young man stopped.

"That one?"

"Yes."

McGee opened the car door with a sigh. He raised his
foot to step inside—but he did not take that step. The
reason was a forcible blow that caught McGee suddenly,
without warning on the back of the head.

It came swiftly—first a soft hiss in the night, behind
McGee. Sensing a movement behind him, half twisting,
he saw something black dart toward him. He saw nothing else before the blow took him just above the ear—a
stinging, blinding shock that sent him spilling backwards!

A hoarse shout came from Brad Selden—McGee heard
it as he struck the ground, as the night grew thicker around
him. He struggled to get up, but his weakened arms would

not support him; and as he tried he heard gruff commands beside the car. Suddenly he heard the grinding of a starter, the spurt of a motor, and the gritting of wheels on the driveway.

That brought McGee back to himself. He pulled up, while the world spun about him. Through bleared eyes he saw the red light of the car as it sped toward the gate. Confusedly McGee dragged out his gun, aimed, fired....

The report was like another blow on his throbbing head. The other car whirled through the gateway, its speed undiminished, twisted onto the road, roared off....

McGee stumbled toward the police sedan, boiling with rage.

Behind him he heard a door open and slam. Quick footfalls came across the lawn.

"Show-Me! Hey, Show-Me!"

Baxter. Cursing, McGee fumbled the key about in the ignition lock, stamped on the starter, snapped the shift-lever. Baxter sprang around the car, jumped onto the running-board as it started. McGee sent the sedan whizzing toward the gate as Baxter scrambled in.

"Who shot? What happened?"

"Somebody's grabbed young Selden!" McGee snapped. "I was taking him down—but somebody rapped me on the head and grabbed him!"

"Somebody? You mean Brad Selden rapped you?"

"No, damn it! No! Somebody else—got me from behind—I don't know who!"

The tires whined as McGee spun the car into the road. His head was clearing now; at least he could see. The road stretched straight ahead, a white ribbon; and a mile away was the glaring red gleam of a tail light. That was the car he wanted—the car that was carrying Brad Selden and the man who had hit McGee....

The motor of the police car roared at the limit of its power as McGee sent it whizzing over the road—his gaze fast on that spot of red....

4

WARNING BY WIRE

SUDDENLY McGEE HEAVED against the brake pedal. The police car shuddered to a slower speed. Baxter gripped the door, edged forward. McGee stared ahead at the spot of red flying over the road.

"What're you stopping for?" Baxter blurted. "They'll get away!"

The car was still moving, but still slowing. McGee pushed his head out the window, sniffed of the air.

"I smell smoke!"

"Show-Me! Step on it! They're getting out of sight!"

McGee saw that. The car ahead was swinging around a bend in the road. Its tail light was flickering through the bordering trees, disappearing. Still McGee kept his foot on the brake pedal.

"I've been smelling smoke for the past mile! No ordinary smoke, either! It smells like—"

McGee's last word was drowned out by a wailing screech of the brakes as the sedan slid to a complete stop. Swiftly he dislodged himself from the wheel, threw the door open, hopped out. Again he glanced ahead—and saw that the tail light of the other car had vanished!

"Show-Me, come on! We'll never catch 'em!" Baxter
wailed.

McGee scarcely heard. He was staring at the side of the
car. Into the beams of the headlamps came a gust of thin
smoke! Suddenly he lowered himself to his knees, and
peered under the car.

In the darkness he saw a spot of red, like the glowing
end of a cigarette. But it was a live thing—hissing, throwing off flashing sparks!

McGee leaped to his feet.

"Get out of that car!" he yelled.

Baxter was staring at him. "What the hell? You gone
nuts? Show-Me, we've got to catch—"

"Get out of there, Box-Car! For the love of Heaven, get
out of there!"

The frantic ring in McGee's voice stirred Baxter. But he
moved too slowly to suit McGee. The big detective sprang
away, darted past the front of the car, flung open the opposite door, grabbed Baxter's arm.

"Move, for God's sake!"

He gave a pull that spilled Baxter out precipitately.
McGee moaned; he yanked again, jerking Baxter to an
upright position. Then he started away, along the side of the
road, running for all he was worth, pulling Baxter with him.
The younger detective stumbled breathlessly, but McGee
did not lose speed.

They were a hundred yards away when it happened.

A terrific concussion shook the night! Heaven and earth
were suddenly lighted by a blinding glare of orange-white
flame. The force of a thousand lightning-bolts seemed to
strike the road in an instant!

McGee yelled and flung himself down. Baxter spilled on top of him, gasping. McGee managed one glance backward as he fell—a glance toward the police sedan. He saw the blast of fire engulfing it, poisonous smoke gusting up!

The next instant the flash was gone. The thunderous report rolled away into the distance… Through the churning air came a rain of invisible things.

McGee twisted about, sat up. Baxter came to his knees. They stared along the road toward the spot where they had left the sedan.

It had been flung aside like a fragile toy. Its headlamps were out. Its motor had stopped. Tongues of flame were playing along its bursted top. One of its rear wheels lay in the grass, the other on the edge of the road. In an instant the police car had been turned into an utter wreck—like the cars of Cornelius and Fletcher Selden!

WRATHFULLY AND BREATHLESSLY McGee loped toward it. Baxter followed him, taking in gulps of acrid air. They stared a moment; they dug their fingers into loose earth and flung it on the flames. The fire smothered out; thick smoke poured up. Backing away, they regarded the misshapen vehicle.

"God! If we'd been in it!" Baxter exclaimed.

"If we'd been in it, we'd be mincemeat now!" McGee snapped.

He glanced around quickly. The road was dark; the car that had carried off Brad Selden must be far ahead. There was no house in sight. McGee quickly grabbed Baxter's arm, pulled him away.

"We've got to beat it back!"

He trotted along the road, in the direction of the Selden

place. Baxter ran beside him, still stunned. McGee puffed; sweat ran down his face as he kept chugging. Baxter peered into the sky, all around, and listened.

"Show-Me, there wasn't any plane above our car that time!"

"Damn' right there wasn't!" McGee blurted. "We can't blame that explosion on any plane!"

"What!"

"Nope! The thing that blew up that car was a charge of dynamite hidden under it!"

Baxter was panting. "Dynamite under it! What the hell? How did it get there? Who set it off? How do you know—"

McGee kept trotting. "What I smelled was the fuse burning. When I looked under, I saw it—a piece of fuse hanging down right under my seat! The dynamite must've been fastened under the floor boards—enough to blow us both to Kingdom Come and then some!"

Baxter thought that over, appalled, as he ran. "But, good gosh, Show-Me! That was your car! Do you suppose the dynamite was put in it while you were at Selden's place?"

"I don't suppose anything!" McGee snapped. "Except that the guy behind this is hell-bent on blowing a lot of people to smithereens!"

Now they saw a light ahead—a light shining through a window of the Selden house. They reached the gate, jogged through. The moon lighted their way as they followed the path toward the house. Suddenly Baxter exclaimed: "Hey, Show-Me! The other police car's gone—the one I brought! The guy that grabbed Brad Selden must've used it!"

McGee stopped, stared, saw that in fact Baxter's official car had disappeared! With an angry grunt, he headed for the broken French window, hopped through, skirted around the ragged hole in the floor, and darted into the living room.

He saw that Diane Holland was still there; but he gave her scant attention. He grabbed up the telephone, barked "Police Headquarters!"

Baxter had followed. Twisting, McGee asked him: "You know the license number on that crate, Box-Car?"

"No!"

McGee moaned, shook the telephone as if to hurry the call. Suddenly he sang out:

"Sullivan! McGee. Now, by damn, we've got a kidnaping on top of two murders! Brad Selden was just grabbed! Some guy carried him off in a police car. I said 'a police car,' damn it, yes! Baxter had it. Signal every prowl car in town, Sully—tell 'em to look for the car that's carrying Brad Selden!

"Phone Townland—it was heading that way! Get Curtisville on the wire, and Huntington, and Proctor. The car may try to get through those places—if it does it's got to be stopped! You know what to do—do it! Fast!"

McGee lowered the phone, took a deep breath. Diane Holland was gazing at him widely.

"What's happened to Brad?" she asked suddenly.

"Kidnaped, like I said! At least, it looks like he was kidnaped."

Baxter was breathing hard. "What'll we do now, Show-Me? Both cars're gone!"

"You may use mine," Diane Holland answered quickly. "I brought Brad from the airport in it. I'll stay here tonight— you're free to use my car if you like."

"Thanks! We will!" McGee answered. He started for the French door and paused again. "Damn' if I know what's behind all this, but don't you worry," he added.

Suddenly the telephone rang.

"But Brad's father and brother were both killed—and now Brad—" The girl broke off, hysterically.

The telephone shrilled again.

"Probably Sullivan," McGee said, and moved toward it. "There's no use getting in a lather," he told the girl. "You pull yourself together!"

As he clamped the receiver to his ear he was startled to hear a high-pitched, crazy laugh. "Hello!"

The laughter stopped abruptly. A nasal voice came over the wire.

"Detective McGee? My apologies, if you please."

"Apologies?" McGee snapped. "What for? Who's talking?"

"For rapping you on the head," the voice twanged back. "I'm sorry, but it was necessary. You needn't worry about young Selden yet—if you behave sensibly."

McGee took a tighter grip on the phone. His heart was pounding; he decided to spar for time.

"Speak louder! I can't hear you!"

"Yes you can, McGee. You can hear me perfectly. It won't do you any good to trace this call. I'll tell you now it's coming from a pay-phone at the crossroads halfway to Townland. I may say, too, that I'm really rather glad you didn't get killed when your car exploded."

McGee's knuckles went white, his neck red. "Listen!" he barked. "You can't get away with this! If you've got Brad

Selden with you—I warn you to let him go right now!
We'll find out who you are and where you are—and—"

"Who I am?" the twanging voice interrupted. "Don't you
know, McGee? My name is Zorda—A. Zorda. I live at 30
Eternity Street. There is no such place, but that's where I
live. The numeral thirty, you know, is a telegrapher's symbol
for 'the end.' Clever, don't you think?"

McGee glared around helplessly. "This guy's crazy!" he
muttered.

The sinister voice dropped to a lower tone. "I'm warning
you, McGee. Don't try to find me. Don't try to stop me.
I have killed two of the Selden family, and if there is the
slightest police interference, I'll kill a third. It's my revenge,
McGee—death to the Seldens! And death for you if you
don't let me alone!"

McGee gulped: said nothing.

"That's my promise, McGee. Revenge! Death!"

And again, over the wire, came a horrible, insane chuck-
ling. Suddenly it broke off—as the line went dead....

McGee slammed the phone down.

"Zorda! Somebody calling himself Zorda! Warning us
to keep hands off! The place he phoned from is ten miles
from here at least—he'll be the hell and gone before we
can get there!"

He grabbed up the phone again, again called Police
Headquarters.

"Sullivan! Just got a warning from the guy who kidnaped
young Selden! He phoned from the crossroads halfway to
Townland. Any prowl cars out that far?..." McGee moaned
again. "I thought not! Get the dope from the phone
company, Sully—some store out there! Get a description

if you can! Send the prowl cars out! I'm beating it there myself right now!"

Again he abandoned the phone, and hurried to the French doors. Baxter followed him uncertainly. Diane Holland was gazing at him in terror. McGee paused, shot a question at her:

"The guy who just phoned said something about revenge—vengeance on the Seldens. Do you know anybody who might have reason for hating the Seldens so much—"

"No. Of course not," the girl said dazedly.

"Sure?"

"I've known the Seldens all my life. Finer people never lived. They have never hurt anybody—in business or in any other way. They've given hundreds of thousands to charity. They—they're the fairest, most generous people on earth. No one could possibly have any reason for hating them. It—it's absurd!"

"Well—" said McGee skeptically.

Suddenly he turned, hurried out of the house, and ran toward the long, sleek roadster that belonged to Diane Holland. Clambering in, he found the key in the ignition lock. Baxter fell into the seat beside McGee as the car began to roll.

McGee shot it toward the gateway. "Any cop who believed everything he heard in this case would certainly go nuts!" he snapped as the roadster swung onto the road....

5

HOW DEATH CAME

IT WAS LATE in the afternoon of the next day when McGee turned Diane Holland's roadster through the gate of the Selden estate and brought it to a stop beside the garage. Baxter was with him: both of them looked exhausted and disheartened.

As he climbed out, McGee saw Diane Holland hurrying toward them from the house. He sighed, eyed the girl sympathetically, and sighed again. She stopped, gazing at him wordlessly.

"Miss Holland," he said, "there's no news. We haven't found Brad. We don't know where he is, or who grabbed him."

The girl asked: "Haven't you any hope—"

"We've got all the hope in the world of finding him," McGee answered slowly, "but I'm buffaloed. As soon as I get an idea on this case, it goes to pieces. Just you keep a stiff upper lip, that's all."

The girl nodded, slowly. McGee saw that she was laboring under a terrific strain. He tried to think of something to say.

"Good car," he observed, patting the fender of the roadster. "Only you don't get good mileage. The ads say you'll get twelve, but we only got eight to the gallon. You can't believe anything you read in advertisements."

The girl turned away, hurried toward the house to hide the tears that welled to her eyes. McGee sighed again, and looked around. He sat on the running board of the roadster.

"Now I've got time to take a breath and check up, Box-Car," he said musingly. "Let's see. The guy who grabbed Brad Selden had it all planned. We found the police sedan abandoned about a mile from here on a side road, which means he parked his own bus there and came on foot. Grabbed the police car, got away, circled, changed cars, and took to cover. Naturally none of the prowl busses spotted him."

"Yeah," said Baxter wearily.

"And that's as far as we go," McGee continued. "Well, I've got another idea, Box-Car. See you in a minute."

He got up, trudged to the house, and went inside. In the living room he picked up the telephone and thumbed through the directory. Selecting a number, he put through a call.

"Lambert Airplane Factory? Is Mr. Lambert there?"

In a moment Edgar Lambert was on the wire.

"McGee talking, Lambert. We've been hunting for Brad Selden all day, and haven't found him. The prowl cars have done as much as they can do, but we haven't got anywhere. How about using an airplane?"

"Good idea, McGee," Lambert answered. "I'm at your service. I'll put as many planes as you want at your disposal."

"One'll be enough," McGee judged. "Young Selden can't be very far away. He's probably hidden in some out-of-the-way place off the main roads. We'll be able to spot places like that from the air without any trouble. Suppose we take a spin all around this side of town, and see if we can find anything that looks like a hideaway."

"Certainly," Lambert answered. "We've still got several hours of daylight. I'm ready to start immediately. I can pilot you myself."

"Okay. How'll I connect with you?"

"There's plenty of open space on the Selden grounds to make a landing. I've done it often, and so has Brad. I'll hop over as soon as I get a plane warmed."

McGee grunted approval, put down the phone, and trudged out of the house. He returned to the roadster to find Baxter seated on the runningboard, deep in thought. Baxter looked up and said:

"I had a theory, but—"

"Theories can't be trusted," McGee stated. "Of all the things that can't be trusted in this world, theories are at the bottom of the list… I'm going to take a look around."

McGee sighed, and started for the garage. It was an unusually large structure, large enough for the storage of four cars. Stepping inside, McGee found it empty, solidly built and clean. He crossed to a tool bench which ran along one wall, pulled open its drawers, poked inside, and shut them. From the doorway Baxter watched.

"Hunting for something in particular, Show-Me?"

"Maybe. You had the right dope last night, Box-Car. The dynamite was probably put under our sedan while it was setting here on the grounds. The Seldens' two cars exploded the same way, so they were probably fixed here, too."

Now McGee was probing under the bench. He moved an oil barrel and peered behind it. He opened a closet and found suits of coveralls hanging inside—nothing suspicious. He paused, looked around again, and moved toward several partly-worn tires which were hanging from stout nails on the wall.

Either the dynamite was kept somewhere around here, or a supply of it was brought in," he observed, reaching up. "There may be no way of telling what—" He broke off suddenly. "Hello!"

He had his hand around one of the extra tires and was pinching it. Inside he felt something hard, unyielding. Quickly he fingered the tire open, peered into its interior.

"Looka that!" he blurted.

McGee pulled something out of the hollow interior of the tire as Baxter bent over to watch. He held it in his hand, staring at it. It was three sticks of dynamite, tied together, with a long fuse protruding from one of them!

"Good gosh!"

McGEE'S FACE WAS grim. He ran his hand along the length of fuse and peered at the end of it. He found half a dozen kitchen matches fastened to the end of the fuse with twisted wire! Their shanks were bound tightly; their colored heads protruded slightly beyond the end of the fuse!

"That did it!" McGee exclaimed.

McGee pushed his hand into the interior of the tire again; this time he brought out a small coil of stovepipe wire. Quickly he raised, turned, felt of the other tires hanging against the wall. They responded to the squeeze of his hand; he found nothing else in any of them. Turning, he glared at Baxter.

"That did it, Box-Car! That's the way it was worked! The

dynamite was fastened under the floor boards of the cars, maybe to a brake rod or a cross bar! Then the end of the fuse was wired to the exhaust pipe! God, what a devilish way to kill a man!"

Baxter's eyes were wide. "I get it! The fuse wouldn't ignite until after the car was started. As soon as the car ran away, the exhaust pipe got hot and set off the matches. The flame of the matches ignited the fuse. The fuse burned back to the dynamite and—blooey!"

"Blooey, Box-Car," said McGee grimly, "is right! That's how it worked! The devil! There wasn't any way of finding out about how the dynamite was fixed afterward! We saw the plane overhead both times, and I assumed it'd dropped a bomb, when all the time the car was carrying the dynamite right with it!

"See how it worked? The murderer didn't have to be anywhere around at the time the dynamite went off! He sneaked in here and fastened the dynamite under both of the Selden cars, knowing that they'd explode on the way to town the next morning. The Seldens didn't have a chance! They were sitting right on top of the dynamite all the time!"

"And so were we!" Baxter gulped.

"I'll say we were! If I hadn't smelled the fuse burning— The murderer came back the next night, put the dynamite under our car. Trying to stop us from finding out something, maybe—desperate! And he hid this extra charge in the old tire. God, is he planning to blow up somebody else? Is he—"

McGee broke off, frowning. He looked around, and up. He waited a minute, silent.

"How does that figure?" Baxter asked breathlessly. "Our

car was all set to blow up, and you were taking Brad Selden
to it to drive him to Headquarters and—"

"Listen!" McGee snapped.

He looked around again; and this time Baxter heard
the sound that had attracted McGee's attention. It was
faint—a vague thumping. Its source was uncertain. The
noise vanished; then it came again.

Three dull thumps....

McGee peered at the ceiling. Plainly, there was some
sort of enclosed space above—perhaps a storage room. At
one side of the ceiling was a separate section: a broad crack
showed. A rope was stapled to one corner of that section; it
passed over a pulley in the upper corner of the garage; and
it was taut with the weight of a number of sash-weights
fastened to its lower end.

McGee crossed to that corner quickly. He lifted the
sash-weights slowly, and a section of the ceiling began
to drop on hinges. When it was halfway down McGee
grasped it, pulled it lower. The upper side of the section
was a short flight of steps; the whole trap was counterbal-
anced by the iron.

The sound came more loudly: thump, thump!

McGee's eyes were narrowed, cautious. His hand moved
toward his hip pocket holster as he began to climb the
stairs. Baxter followed him closely... When his head was
above the level of the ceiling, McGee paused, looked
around. Suddenly an exclamation escaped him; he sprang
up.

The space above the garage ceiling was low, lighted by
two dormer windows, half filled with articles of furniture
in bad repair. But it was none of the stored stuff that star-

tled McGee. His gaze fastened on the figure of a man lying on the dusty floor!

The man was lying on his side; his head and shoulders were completely covered with a burlap bag, tied in place. His hands were bound behind him; his ankles were fastened!

"Love of Heaven!" McGee blurted.

The bound man on the floor wriggled. No sound came from the heavy burlap covering his head save a stifled breathing. As he moved, his heels thumped the flooring—the sound McGee had heard....

Hastily McGee stooped, tore at the cord which fastened the burlap bag in place. The strand broke; McGee dragged the thing off.

"God's sake!" he sang out.

It was Brad Selden!

THE LOWER HALF of young Selden's face was covered with a tightly-knotted handkerchief holding a gag in place. His eyes were frantic, pleading. One stupefied moment McGee hesitated; then he jerked out his pocketknife, cut the handkerchief from Brad Selden's face, removed the gag.

Brad Selden gasped, drew in a deep breath, as McGee cut the ropes that bound him. He fell back, exhausted; suddenly he pulled himself up, panting.

"Hey!" Baxter blurted. "We've been hunting for you all day! How the hell—"

Selden was staring around in amazement. "I'm—this is the attic of our garage!" he interrupted breathily.

"Didn't you know where you were?" McGee demanded.

"No! I had no idea! I heard you talking below—I thought you'd found me—I kicked the floor. Lord—I—"

"You must be hungry and thirsty as the devil, and all worn out," McGee said sympathetically, "but I've got to ask you some more damn-fool questions. Who was the man who grabbed you?"

Selden rubbed his abused mouth. "I don't know. I didn't see his face. I saw him sneak up behind you—he had a handkerchief tied across his face. Then he hit me with a gun, pulled the bag over my head, and pushed me into the car."

"Got any idea where he went? Any idea at all who he is?"

"I was too dizzy to tell where we were going, and I couldn't see. Whoever it was, he didn't even speak. When I began to come around, he tied me up; then he transferred me to another car. It must've been late last night when he brought me here, but I didn't know where I was."

McGee picked up the two handkerchiefs: the one had gagged the young man, the other had fastened the gag in place. He sought marks on them, something to help identify the owner. They were perfectly plain, unmarked.

"Well," McGee sighed, "one more question. Have you got any idea *why* this bird grabbed you?"

"No."

Brad Selden came to his feet as McGee scowled.

"Just afterward, a guy called on the phone, gave his name as A. Zorda, and threatened to kill you if we interfered. Said it was a plan of revenge on the Selden family. Miss Holland says the idea is absurd, but you may know of something in connection with the family that she doesn't. Better come out with it—it's important."

Selden looked puzzled. "It *is* absurd," he answered. "Revenge on Dad—Fletcher? It's unthinkable. They've never done anything to make anyone hate them. No depositor in Dad's bank has ever lost a cent; he's been very lenient on notes and foreclosures.

"Fletcher—why, once Fletch sponsored a sale of bonds, and when the company defaulted, Fletch paid up out of his own pocket. Men like that can't be hated."

"I'll say not," McGee sighed. "Maybe this Zorda guy is crazy enough to imagine something, but—I don't know."

McGee paced across the storage space and back while young Selden rubbed his swollen wrists and ankles.

Baxter offered: "This guy Zorda threatened to kill you, Selden—yet he brought you right back home. He put you here, where he couldn't reach you again without running a big risk. It almost looks like he *wanted* somebody to find you here—but why—"

McGee turned. "I'm 'way ahead of you, Box-Car, 'way ahead. This may be a Chinese puzzle to you, but I'm beginning to see the light. I—" He stopped abruptly, faced Selden. "Listen. I want help from you."

"Certainly," Selden said. "Anything I can do will be little enough—after—"

"Okay. You're safe and sound here—and I want you to stay here. Right here in the attic of this garage. I want you to keep out of sight. The idea is this: I don't want anybody to know you've been found."

"Diane—"

"It may be tough on her, but it won't be for long. This idea of mine may not be worth much—I don't trust ideas—but I'm going to try it out. All you have to do is stay hidden here. Okay?"

"Yes," Selden said uncertainly.

"**BOX-CAR AND I** are going right down again. If there happens to be any excitement around here, you keep as quiet as a mouse. You'll be all right. Understand?"

Selden didn't, but he nodded. McGee signalled Baxter, went to the stairs and trod down them. When Baxter's weight was off the section, McGee lifted it, swung it up, then closed the trap completely by pulling on the counterweighted rope.

"What's the grand idea, Show-Me?" Baxter asked curiously.

McGee fixed him with a stern eye and said quietly: "Don't ask!"

The dynamite was lying on the floor where McGee had left it. He picked it up, tucked it gently back into the worn tire, then replaced the tire on its nail.

He crossed to a corner and peered at a telephone instrument affixed to the wall. His inspection showed him that it was connected with the house. He lifted the receiver, heard a hum that meant the line was working, and replaced it.

From the opposite corner he lifted a large galvanized can. Bringing it to the center of the garage, he dumped out its contents. A pile of greasy cotton waste fell to the cement floor. McGee quietly returned the can to its place and looked around again.

On the rear wall a copper fire extinguisher was hanging from a rack. McGee lifted it down, left it near the wall.

He went to the doors and folded them almost shut, leaving a crack wide enough to wriggle through. He sidled out, and Baxter followed.

"You're not being mysterious, are you, Show-Me?" Baxter asked wryly.

McGee conducted Baxter a short distance from the garage and they talked in whispers.

"Now, Box-Car, I want you to do exactly as I say. A lot depends on it. Be sure you get everything straight. Did you notice that little telephone?"

"Yes, but—"

"You saw that pile of old waste on the floor?"

"Yes, but—"

"You saw that fire extinguisher?"

"Yes, but—"

"I want you to go into the garage when I get through telling you what to do, and close the door—tight. Don't do a thing until you hear that telephone ring. Don't answer the phone—I won't want to talk with you—it'll only be a signal.

"When you hear the signal, strike a match and set fire to that waste in the middle of the floor. Make it a good, smoky fire. Better open the window so a lot of smoke'll come pouring out. Don't suffocate yourself, but let that waste burn."

"What?" Baxter exclaimed. "With that dynamite still in there? You want me to be blown clear to—"

"I tell you you've got to do it!" McGee snapped. "Keep that fire burning until I tell you to put it out. Then turn the extinguisher on it. I don't want to damage the garage, or you either, Box-Car, but—"

"I've got it!" Baxter's eyes were shining. "You figure that in spite of everything, Brad Selden is the murderer. He's the only one who would profit by the death of his brother and father. You want to find out if he hid the dynamite in the garage? He'll figure the fire is a real one, and he'll be afraid the dynamite will explode, so he'll try to get it out—show he's the one who put it there!"

"Have it your own way, Box-Car, but watch yourself!" McGee warned. "Keep out of sight. If Selden comes down from upstairs, or if anybody comes in from outside, duck. Got that?"

"Okay!"

McGee turned his eyes into the sky toward the west. He patted Baxter's shoulder impatiently.

"Now get in there and close the door and play dead until you hear the phone ring!"

Baxter complied with alacrity. McGee made sure the garage doors were shut, then peered again into the western sky.

An airplane was dropping out of the blue, growing larger in perspective, sliding down to a landing on the broad field at the rear of the Selden house.

6

THE MAN FROM MISSOURI

THE AIRPLANE, A trim cabin job, touched three points and ran smoothly toward the house. It slowed to a stop, but its propeller continued to spin as the door of the plane opened and Edgar Lambert hopped out.

McGee strode to meet him. Lambert was clothed in ordinary attire; neither jacket nor helmet was necessary in the closed plane. He gripped McGee's hand and said hurriedly:

"All set. We can hop immediately, if you're ready."

"Not quite," McGee answered. "I've got to call Headquarters. I'll be right with you."

He turned and strode toward the house with Lambert following. As he entered, he passed Diane Holland. He strode into the living room, and heard the girl talking with Lambert outside. On the rear wall was one of the small inter-house telephones. McGee stepped to it.

He lifted the receiver, pushed the red button labelled *Garage,* then punched the bell-button and returned the receiver to its hook.

He picked up the outside telephone, called Headquarters, and got Sullivan.

"Any dope, Sully? Any fingerprints on that police car the kidnaper used?"

"A mess of 'em, but they all belong to cops," Sullivan answered.

"Nothing else?"

"Nope. The kidnaper must have used gloves, as you might expect."

"Looks like rain," McGee remarked, "and the papers this morning said 'Fair' again."

He hung up, walked through the French window, and found Lambert still talking with the girl. She turned to McGee impulsively.

"You're going to hunt for Brad from the air," she said. "I'm going with you."

"I'd rather you didn't," McGee told her.

"But—I can't stay here, any more, doing nothing! I want to do something to help! The cabin job is big enough so I won't be in the way. I've got to come along."

"I see no harm in letting her come, McGee," Lambert smiled.

"Aw, well, all right," McGee said.

He turned, started to walk away from the house. Suddenly he paused, his head coming up sharply. He blurted:

"Looka that! Fire!"

Lambert turned quickly; an exclamation came from Diane's lips; and the three of them peered toward the garage.

Thick, black smoke was pouring from the open window of the garage! It gushed out, tore away on the wind, sooty

and heavy. Behind the greasy panes flames were visible—
long red tongues of fire leaping up!

"What the devil!" McGee exclaimed with simulated
surprise.

He started on an abrupt run toward the building.
Lambert came behind him, loping. As they moved, the
volume of smoke streaming through the window became
greater. The red gleam through the blackened panes made
it seem that the whole interior of the garage was a furnace
of flame.

Diane Holland was following. "There's an extinguisher
inside!" she called as McGee and Lambert hurried on.

McGee led the way, swinging his legs heavily. When he
reached the door of the garage he hesitated. Inside was an
ominous roaring and hissing. McGee suddenly jerked at
the doors, folded one of them partly back.

A terrific gust of smoke burst out, enveloping him. He
leaped back choking. Through the doorway he could see
the swirling mass of flame, and the heat beat out at him.

"Can't get through that!" he gasped.

Lambert was crowding beside McGee, staring in.
Abruptly he thrust McGee aside, started for the partly
opened door. McGee whirled, caught Lambert's arm,
pulled him back.

"Don't go in there!" he blurted. "That smoke'll blind you
in a minute—knock you out!"

Lambert paused. He was pale; his eyes were wide, shining with a strange desperation.

"Better get away from here!" McGee exclaimed. "There
may be gasoline in there—it'll explode!"

Lambert's eyes became filled with a wild light. He

turned back, suddenly, toward the door. As he started in, McGee again caught him.

"You can't go in! Do you want—"

Lambert twisted savagely, thrust McGee away. "Keep your hands off!"

McGee lurched back under the force of Lambert's push. Lambert whirled again, stiffened himself—and suddenly darted inside! He disappeared in the billowing smoke—darting toward the rear wall!

McGee thrust the door wider and, as a greater torrent of smoke poured out, plunged in. Covering his nose and mouth with his bent arm, he crouched, peering. The heat of the flames was terrific; but in the dancing, grotesque light, McGee could see Lambert groping along the wall, at the spot where the fire-extinguisher had hung....

Lambert found the hook empty, looked around wildly; and from his lips came an agonized "Oh, God!"

McGee, kneeling to escape the thickest smoke, peered around. He blessed Baxter for having dragged the extinguisher out of sight. He caught a glimpse of something black and moving behind an oil barrel in the corner. That was Baxter, following orders in spite of the torture the smoke must be inflicting upon him... And beside the barrel stood the extinguisher.

McGee's smarting eyes jerked back to Lambert. Lambert was groping on. His hands struck the tire hanging on the wall—the tire which hid the explosive. A satisfied exclamation came from McGee as he watched—watched Lambert pull the dynamite out of its hiding place, spin about, grope toward the door.

McGee backed out as Lambert stumbled into the air.

Lambert paused as if in a stupor; a cough shook him; he blinked through streaming eyes and laid the dynamite on the ground. McGee's eyes were narrowed; he was reaching for his automatic. And suddenly Lambert turned, dashed into the smoke-filled garage again.

Grimly McGee grasped the wide doors, thrust them open wider. Air gusted in; fumes spewed out. Lambert was springing toward the side wall of the garage. He grasped the counterweighted rope, tugged it upward. As the section of stairway began to unfold, he reached up crazily, slammed it down.

He stared up.

"Brad!" he choked. "Brad!"

McGee had seen enough. He raced across the garage, reached the base of the steps as Lambert was halfway up them. He groped upward for Lambert's legs, and at that instant Lambert stopped suddenly. "Brad!"

YOUNG SELDEN'S FACE was visible in the greasy fumes— looking down from the space above the ceiling.

McGee's left hand gripped Lambert's ankle.

"Get out of here, Lambert! Quick!"

Lambert stared down, a crazy light shining in his eyes. He saw the grim set of McGee's face, the gun in McGee's hand. He stared again at Brad, dumfounded.

Over his shoulder McGee yelled: "Put it out, Box-Car! Put the fire out!"

Lambert looked down again, dimly saw Baxter hurrying from the corner, dragging the fire extinguisher. Baxter ducked near the flames, turning the extinguisher upside down. From the nozzle came a stream of hissing spray.

White steam mixed with the black smoke as the fluid drenched the flaming waste.

McGee, peering grimly up at Lambert, snapped: "You bit, guy! Come down!"

A hoarse rattling sound came from Lambert's throat as he whirled. One instant he poised; he flung himself forward wildly. McGee saw the move, but the surprise of it caught him motionless. Lambert leaped—flinging himself down on top of McGee!

Lambert's weight struck McGee on the chest and shoulders. He gasped, groped for a hold on the stairs, missed. Swiftly he toppled back, Lambert bearing him down, clinging to him like a wildcat. McGee made a swift pass with his gun, aiming for Lambert's head. Instantly his own head struck the cement floor.

McGee moaned, went lax—fought to retain consciousness. "Stop him!" he tried to yell to Baxter, but his voice was only a moan. He twisted, tried to get up. The heady smoke, the violence of the blow, made him reel. As he staggered toward the door, he heard a shot—another—and Baxter shouting....

McGee stumbled into clear air, staring past the garage. Lambert was running wildly toward the plane which had brought him. The plane!

Baxter levelled his automatic, fired. Lambert was leaping from side to side crazily; the bullet missed. McGee ran forward, stopped, flung up his own gun. Three times he pulled the trigger, trying to aim with eyes that scarcely saw. Choking, sobbing, he lowered the gun.

Lambert was out of range now. He was scrambling through the cabin door of the plane. McGee started to run dizzily toward it. The next moment the motor of the plane snarled; the propeller flashed; the plane began to rush across the ground into the takeoff!

McGee took another wrathful shot at it, cursed himself for trying, whirled to Baxter.

"Get to the phone, Box-Car! Phone Sullivan! Tell him to warn every landing field around here! Get the prowl cars on the job—everything! Snap it up! We'll get that guy!"

Baxter stared. "Sure—sure," he mumbled. "He's the guy, all right. But why—what would *he* get out of killing—"

"*Move!*"

Baxter moved—raced toward the house. McGee whirled about. The fire inside the garage was out. Brad Selden had hurried down the stairs; Diane Holland was clinging to him, sobbing. McGee stared at the ground—looking for the dynamite that Lambert had brought out.

It was gone!

"He must've taken it! I'll get that guy!"

He ran swiftly toward the girl's roadster, peering into the air, at the plane rushing across the sky. Swiftly he started the motor, threw the roadster into gear. As he swung about, Brad Selden caught hold, pulled himself up, tumbled into the seat.

"You can't keep up with him in a car!"

"I know it, damn it! But I can keep him in sight longer!"

McGee shot the roadster toward the gate. He veered through it, turned on two wheels onto the cement highway. Staring up, he gave the motor the limit of the accelerator. Lambert's plane was flying dead away, still climbing.

"You're taking a chance!" Selden gasped. "He's got that

dynamite! If he knows you're following him, he might drop it on you!"

"According to Lambert, that's not so easy to do!" McGee snapped. "He knows that hiding the stuff under the car is easier! He did it—he made those cars blow up!"

McGEE SENT THE roadster swinging swiftly around a bend. His eyes flickered up and down as he twisted the wheel. The plane was still nosing directly away—its speed increasing....

"He hasn't got a chance!" McGee snapped. "If he comes down at any airport he'll be grabbed. If he doesn't, it'll be easy enough to spot him. He won't be able to get away!"

Brad Selden was peering at the plane grimly. "I didn't suspect it was Lambert. I didn't know—"

"I got the dope on that bird today!" McGee snapped. "I concentrated on him because it was the only angle that was possible. You didn't have any reason for killing your father and brother. There wasn't any place else to look! Lambert had a reason, all right!"

The tires whined as McGee took another curve. Brad Selden stared at him.

"He had—"

"A damn' good one. He supplied you with your planes. I found out that three of your crates'd crashed, that you'd got others from him. You hadn't paid him for any of them— he trusted you, of course—took a mortgage on the field. Between thirty and forty thousand each, those planes— and eight of 'em unpaid for!

"You wouldn't take help from anybody—you wanted to make a go of the field on your own hook—and you were damn' near going into bankruptcy. If you went broke, it meant Lambert wouldn't be able to collect. And if he couldn't collect from you—he was ruined himself. He wanted you to get the money from your Dad, didn't he?"

McGee was hunched over the wheel, eyes in the sky, driving the straightaway.

"Yes—yes, he did!" Selden exclaimed. "He tried to argue me into it. I refused—flatly. It was a question of honor with me—but God! If I'd known he was so desperate—"

"It wasn't you alone. He was in over his head, trying to make a go of his factory. But if you paid him, he'd be saved. You couldn't do that. Fair enough on your part. Lambert supplied you with ships with his eyes open—he knew the chance he was running. He wasn't man enough to face the deal when things went wrong.

"He figured that the Selden money was coming to you some day. He wanted to hurry it. Once the estate belonged to you, you'd be able to pay off your debt to him, he'd be able to save himself. Killed your father and brother so you could pay him with their money! That guy's a devil!"

The plane in the sky was circling now—turning back! McGee noted the move in amazement. But he kept talking.

"He began working out his plan—but it struck a snag. Why? Because you got yourself suspected of the killings! If you'd been arrested, brought to trial, the settlement of the estate would have been held up—in the meantime Lambert would have been ruined. When you faced trouble, his one concern was to save you.

"That's why he kidnaped you—to save you from arrest. He's A. Zorda. He's the guy who phoned those threats. He didn't mean 'em—his only idea was to convince me that someone else, not you, was guilty. That's the reason for the talk about revenge. Once he pulled suspicion off you, he'd accomplished his purpose—so he brought you back, put you in the garage where you'd be safe.

"Your safety means the success of his plans!"

"Watch it!" Selden exclaimed, peering at the plane. "It's almost above Lambert's own field now!"

"But he's not coming down. He's—"

Surprise choked off McGee's words.

Suddenly the plane in the air split apart! A bright flash of red fire burst out of the cabin! The wings tore off; the fuselage lurched, its nose dropping. Dense smoke poured out of the falling wreckage.

And then the booming report of an explosion reached the ears of McGee and Selden over the roaring of the roadster's motor!

Selden closed his eyes, chilled. McGee stared—stared at the fragments of the plane fluttering down through the air... It was not possible that Lambert was alive now. Not possible....

"He had that dynamite with him!" McGee exclaimed. "He used it—deliberately—because he knew he couldn't get away."

The roadster slowed.

"He knew you had him, McGee," Selden said quietly....

McGEE WALKED FROM the Selden house toward the driveway. A police car was sitting there; it had been brought to the place by McGee's order. Baxter climbed into one side of it; McGee took the wheel.

Brad Selden and Diane Holland, standing close together, watched him solemnly.

"The things that a desperate man will try"—McGee

sighed—"make a hell of a lot of trouble for cops and other folks. If there's anything more I can do, you know you can count on me."

"Thanks, McGee; you've been square," Selden said.

Diane smiled.

"Well," said McGee, "I'm sorry about the inside of the garage. Some fresh paint will brighten it up. Get good paint, though. You can't trust this cheap stuff... Well," he added, "good night."

He swung the car down the driveway, out the gate, and turned it in the direction of Headquarters.

"Show-Me," said Baxter, "you had me fooled. I didn't know you suspected Lambert at all.

"But you had the whole plan figured out, didn't you? All set so that when he arrived you could immediately spring it?"

"Yeah," McGee answered. "That's a fact, Box-Car."

"But why didn't you grab him right away?" Baxter asked as the car sang over the pavement. "If you already knew he was guilty, why did you set the trap for him?"

"Because I had only a theory, and I don't trust theories," McGee answered flatly. "I set the trap for Lambert to make him betray himself—prove beyond any doubt he was the guilty man."

"You didn't believe even your own idea about it?"

McGee wagged his head and gave the motor a bit more gas.

"I'm from Missouri," he said. "Me, I've got to be shown."

MURDER WITHOUT MOTIVE

"Turn Off the Burglar Alarm for Ten Minutes," the Rich Jeweler 'Phoned. In the Morning He Was Missing and Show-Me McGee Had a Big Mystery on His Hands

1

THE WALLS SAW DEATH

A DOOR OPENED on the broad balcony, throwing a shaft of white across the black, silent interior of the store. Two men came through it, the one following the other. Their footfalls sounded on the stairway which led down to the floor of the cavernous room.

This was the establishment of Homer Stratton, Inc., Jewelers. The dim light burning above the black-faced vault in the rear wall disclosed rows of empty glass counters, steel shutters covering the broad street windows. Medieval shields and crossed halberds decorated the walls, and in the corners stood suits of mail, like silent sentinels.

It was almost midnight.

Homer Stratton moved through the empty silence of the store toward the vault. The shine of the globe burning above it darkened the lines in his wizened face, brightened his eyes, made him look like a grim little gnome. The man who followed him watched his every move with cat-like wariness.

Stratton lifted a telephone from a desk. His voice rang hollowly as he asked for a number, as he spoke again:

"Harrison Detective Agency? Homer Stratton talking. I am about to open the main vault in my store. It should remain open not more than ten minutes. Please disconnect the alarm for that length of time, then set it again. That's all; thank you."

Stratton replaced the telephone, stepped to the black metal door, and began to twirl the combination dial. The other man watched him keenly. Back and forth the metal circle spun under pressure of Stratton's lean fingers.

Presently the old jeweler grasped the handle of the vault door and twisted it downward.

He paused. Reflectively he took from his coat pocket a folded sheet of paper. He spread it open and, by the yellow glow of the bulb above him, read:

My dear Stratton:

This will introduce you to Mr. Henry Ritch, an assistant of mine, whom you may implicitly trust. Please turn over to him the Monson collection, and he will give you a receipt for it. It will not take long for me to examine the various pieces, and I will return them to you by Mr. Ritch early tomorrow morning. Thank you very much for the opportunity.

Yours very truly,

Thomas Littlefield.

"One moment," said Homer Stratton thoughtfully.

He returned to the desk, again took up the telephone. The other man turned with eyes sharpening, watching him. Again Stratton's voice echoed from the walls as he called a number.

"Anything wrong?" asked the man in the shadow.

"Just a perfunctory check-up," Stratton answered. "I am phoning Mr. Littlefield to verify his request—his letter."

The woman screamed again—and the armor
plate toppled from its pedestal

"Yes?"

The other man glanced quickly at the vault, noted that the handle was down. His shoulders hunched up, his arms half-bent, as his muscles tightened. His right hand slipped over his vest pocket and withdrew something which looked like a fountain pen. He stepped closer to the desk, pointing it toward the head of Homer Stratton.

"Is that necessary?"

"It's usual."

"Put down that phone!"

Homer Stratton's head turned sharply. "What?"

"Put down that phone!"

The "fountain pen" was directed squarely at Homer Stratton's eyes. The thumb of the man who held it pressed sharply on a small button halfway along its length. The result was a sudden, sharp hiss.

Homer Stratton gasped. Suddenly his eyes were flaming, streaming with scalding tears. He gulped for air, staggered; the phone loosened in his hands. The other man snatched the instrument away, swiftly replacing the receiver.

He stepped back out of the way of the gushing tear gas, as Stratton staggered, groped blindly.

The other man knew exactly what he was doing. His right hand brought from his hip-pocket a heavy automatic. He twirled it, grasped its barrel, and stepped close again. Once he slammed the weighty butt against Homer Stratton's head—twice.

The jeweler moaned, dropped to the floor, lay inert.

Shoulders hunched, the other man retreated from the stinging air about the desk. Swiftly he drew on gloves, turned to the unlocked vault. Before grasping the handle he paused, listening.

Silence....

THE WELL-KNOWN ESTABLISHMENT of Homer Stratton, Inc., was flanked in the rear by an old-fashioned stone-front house. It was Homer Stratton's home, and it connected with the store through a door on the balcony. Its front entrance, on the side-street, was gloomy, unlighted.

Shortly before midnight the door of the Stratton home opened stealthily. A shadowy form crept through, closed the door, made sure the spring lock had caught. The man hurried away, his long legs swinging swiftly.

Halfway down the block he paused at a refuse receptacle provided by the city. The accumulated trash inside rustled as something dropped into it from the hand of the man who had stolen from Homer Stratton's house. He hastened on, past intersections, until he reached an all-night drug-store on a corner.

He stepped inside, sidled into a telephone booth, called a number.

"I've got it," he said, when a voice answered.

"Safe?"

"No—damn it, no! He was about to phone Littlefield and check up on the letter. I had to give it to him."

"What!"

"I tell you, I had to! If he'd reached Littlefield, he would've stepped on an alarm-button and had a couple of prowl cars down there in thirty seconds! What's the differ-ence—I've got it. We're set!"

"You damn fool, as soon as the store opens and they find Stratton—"

"They won't! Give me credit! I've fixed it so we'll have plenty of time to skip. We can be to hell and gone before they even find Stratton. Besides, the police'll go chasing off on a bum steer. I've taken care of everything, I tell you!"

"So *you* say! What about the note?"

The man in the phone booth hesitated in dismay. "The note?"

"The note that got you into the place, idiot! Where is it?"

"Oh, God!" It was a moan of despair. "I left it! It's still there! Stratton put it back in his pocket before I gave him the works!"

"You fool! You damn fool! Don't you know that note can be traced?"

"I had to get out of there! I just had ten minutes—ten minutes for everything—"

"We've got to get that note! We can't let that note fall into the hands of the cops! Go back and get it—right now!"

"I can't!" The man in the booth gasped his protest. "I can't do that! I can't get back in! We've got to let it go. I tell you we've got plenty of time to beat it if—"

"Don't tell me what we're going to do!" snapped the man on the other end of the wire. "You've pulled an idiotic blunder—now I've got to get us out of it. We can't skip until we've tried to get that note back."

"I—I'll do whatever you say! I—"

"You? Let you pull another boner? Not much! Get over here! Right away—understand? Come here right now!"

"Coming."

He slipped out of the telephone booth quickly, pale, trembling. He hurried out of the store, and across the street.

As he disappeared in the shadows the dull booming of a steeple clock shook the air.

Twelve strokes of the gong—midnight....

AT TEN O'CLOCK next morning a girl entered the corner door of Homer Stratton, Inc. She was a very pretty girl, in her early twenties, smartly dressed: but her high color betrayed the fact that she was not at ease; her quick movements testified her anxiety. She walked directly to a counter in the rear of the store, and of the clerk who stepped toward her she inquired:

"Is my pin ready? It was being repaired. Here is my claim-check."

As the clerk went off with her ticket, she raised troubled eyes toward the broad balcony in the rear which overlooked the entire store.

"Show-Me" McGee was on that balcony. He looked like

a detective, and was one. Tall, heavy-set and good-natured, he gazed upon the world with the eyes of a skeptic—keen, gray, unbelieving eyes. Show-Me stuck to John McGee as a nickname because, quite literally, he was from Missouri.

"Pearl necklace gone," he said, scribbling in his notebook, "and another necklace from the Monson collection. How much 're they worth?"

Arthur Stratton answered McGee's question. He was young, handsome, collegiate-looking, the nephew of the owner of the store, and business manager for Homer Stratton, Inc. McGee had come from Headquarters in answer to a summons from Arthur Stratton. James Baxter, detective sergeant, stood at McGee's broad side, listening.

"About twenty thousand on the pearls," Arthur Stratton answered, "and insured. The Monson necklace hasn't much value. It's a good example of French period jewelry, but why the thief took that particular piece is beyond me. There are far more valuable pieces in the Monson collection than that gold necklace."

McGee scribbled.

"It isn't the necklaces that worry me," Stratton went on anxiously. "It's my uncle—Homer Stratton. He's always here promptly when the store opens in the morning. He's very methodical—never goes off schedule. I can't imagine where he is—I *know* something's happened to him."

"Homer Stratton disappeared," McGee mumbled, and wrote it in his notebook....

On the floor below, the girl was still looking up at the balcony. She could see McGee, Baxter and Stratton. She jerked back to herself when the clerk reappeared with the pin she had claimed. Without even inspecting it, she inquired the charge, and paid it.

Nervously, she turned away. But she did not turn toward the outer door. She hurried toward another in the rear of the room, opened it, went in.

Show-Me McGee looked over the railing of the balcony, surveyed the spreading store, its counters now a-glitter with precious stones, silver and gold. With a sigh, he asked:

"There's no sign of your uncle anywhere? He didn't leave a note—didn't say he would be away?"

"Nothing like that," Arthur Stratton answered. "His home is behind the store, you know—that door connects with it. I left Uncle Homer in his library at ten o'clock last night. He said nothing about going away. In fact, as I left, he remarked: 'I'll see you at nine in the morning, as usual, Arthur.'"

"You think maybe he was kidnaped?" McGee asked.

"I don't know!" Stratton exclaimed. "I only know that it's extremely unusual. Evidently Uncle Homer came into the store last night a little after eleven-thirty. When I discovered that the necklaces were missing, I phoned the Harrison Detective Agency immediately. They told me that Uncle Homer had phoned them and asked that the alarm be shut off for ten minutes—that was at eleven thirty-six."

"He opened the safe himself, then, you think?"

"Yes; don't you? Perhaps he took out the necklaces himself. But I don't know why he should have done that. And I can't imagine where he is now. He must have been forced to open the safe by someone who reached him through the house—he must be kidnaped. What do you think, Detective McGee?"

"I'M NOT THINKING yet," McGee answered. "I'm just listening now. Thinking comes later. My old man was a cop, Stratton, and a good one. He used to tell me, 'Son,' he used to say, 'keep an open mind. Don't believe more than one tenth of what you hear, a quarter of what you read, and half of what you see.' That's what he used to say to me."

Stratton looked baffled. "It's all very upsetting. The thief could have taken a hundred thousand dollars' worth of stones if he'd wanted to—but he didn't. He took a pearl necklace valued at about twenty thousand, and the Monson necklace which isn't worth more than five hundred. Why he should overlook the more costly pieces and—what could have happened to Uncle Homer—"

"We," said Show-Me McGee, "will take a look around."

As McGee started down the steps which led to the floor of the store, the door in the farther rear corner opened. The girl came out, looked around quickly, and paused. Opening her purse, she fumbled in it, and moved a step closer toward the suit of armor plate which stood supported on a pedestal in the corner.

Suddenly a shrill scream sang through the store. It rang in McGee's ears as he reached the bottom of the stairs; he twisted quickly, staring. An open aisle led directly across the rear of the store, toward the farther corner in which the girl was standing.

It was the girl who had screamed. Her back was turned; she was rigid, staring at the suit of armor plate; one of her gloved hands was clinging to the metal flap which covered the hip of the steel form. And she screamed again....

As suddenly, the suit of armor plate toppled. Its balance on the pedestal was upset by the unconscious pull the girl gave it. It slumped back against the partition with a clatter; it bent in the middle; it struck the floor with a terrifying crash.

The girl shot one horrified look around the store. Clerks, behind their counters, were staring at her in alarm. Customers were gazing frightenedly. The resounding crash of the falling armor was a nerve-tearing shock. The next instant the young woman broke into a run—a terrified run that took her straight to the door which opened into the street intersection.

"Wait a minute!" shouted Show-Me McGee.

The girl waited neither a minute nor an instant. She was out the door, hurrying along the curb. McGee went after her, his heels pounding. He puffed out of the door just in time to see a taxi jerking from the curb a scant fifty feet away.

Frightened eyes looked back through the rear window of the cab as the taxi sped away—the eyes of the girl who had brought the suit of mail crashing to the floor.

McGee hesitated, puffing. His own car was not far away. His first impulse was to give chase; he started toward his roadster. Automatically, on his photographic memory, the numerals of the taxi's registration plates impressed themselves....

A hoarse shout stopped McGee in his tracks. It came from inside Homer Stratton, Inc., and it was a shout of dismay, of horror. McGee whirled his two hundred pounds, lumbered back through the door, trotted along the aisle which led to the fallen suit of armor.

Arthur Stratton was staring down at it. Detective Jim

Baxter was staring down at it. Half a score of clerks and customers were crowding about, staring down at it.

The force of the crash had flung the visor of the helmet up. Through the opening a face was visible! A wrinkled, old face, with eyes closed—a face spotted with dried blood!

It was the face of Homer Stratton!

"Great gosh—he's dead!" Baxter gulped. "All the time we've been wondering where he was, his body was there in that suit of armor!"

2

THE LOOT COMES BACK

SHOW-ME McGEE GRABBED Baxter's arm.

"Box-Car!" he said. "Get Nelson down here!" Nelson was the medical examiner. "Get Stone!" Stone was the fingerprint expert. "I'm chasing that dame!"

He flung himself along the aisle and out the door. He puffed along the curbing toward his roadster. Then he realized that the taxi which had whirled the girl away had been sitting directly behind his own bus! McGee called down damnation on all taxi-drivers: some of them were far too eager to earn big money by getting people out of scrapes.

As he jerked open the door of his roadster he stopped. Something blue and rectangular lying in the gutter a few yards away struck his eye. Quickly he scooped it up in one immense paw. A woman's purse! It had been lying where the taxi had stood. The pretty young fugitive had dropped it!

McGee took no time to look into the purse then. He wedged himself behind the wheel of his roadster, stamped on the starter, whizzed away from the curb. He shot toward the next intersection with his horn squawking.

How many minutes had passed since the taxi had started away? One at the most! Yet that was time enough. The

streets were full of cars, the sidewalks crowded with pedestrians: the morning shopping period was at its height. The
taxi and the girl might have dodged a dozen different ways.
By now taxi and suspect might be lost in the hubbub of the
downtown section.

It didn't look so good.

An hour later McGee was back, disgruntled. All those
sixty minutes he had spent cruising about the center of
town, trying to spot the taxi or the girl or both. It was
time lost.

He parked his car on the side-street, in front of the home
of the late Homer Stratton, and pulled the blue purse from
his pocket. For the first time he opened it. Perfume came
out of it as he probed into its contents.

A handkerchief—no initial. A compact. A few hairpins.
A coin purse containing $1.61. And a small, folded bit of
paper, McGee spread it out, found words written on it:

> I've got it. Meet me at seven, your place. It's now or never.
>
> I love you, darling.
>
> AS.

"Huh!" commented McGee. "It would seem she was in
on it, all right. Signed, 'AS.' That's funny. Those are Arthur
Stratton's initials."

Skeptic that he was, Show-Me McGee placed not too
much weight upon the cryptic communication. He stuffed
it back into the purse, the purse back into his pocket, and
ambled back into the big jewelry store.

Things had quieted down. The musty, luxurious atmo-
sphere of the place was such that one might never have

suspected anything had happened. McGee trudged up the stairs to the balcony, which served as the establishment's business office.

Arthur Stratton was there, seated at a desk. He looked up, pale, apparently sickened.

"She got away," said McGee. "Can I use your phone?"

HE THOUGHT HE saw a flash of relief shine in young Stratton's eyes; but he wasn't sure. As he called Headquarters and talked, he thought he saw an anxious expression return to Stratton's face; but he wasn't sure of that, either.

"Sullivan," McGee said into the transmitter. "Find me a taxi with the registration number X2-56-98. I want the driver. Oke."

Stratton was peering at him. "Do you think she had anything to do with it?" he asked quickly.

"I'm still not thinking," McGee answered. "But it looks like it. Only, if she is connected with it, why should she come in here, pull that suit of armor over, and scream her head off, and take a chance of getting caught? Know any reason why anybody'd want to kill your uncle?"

Stratton said, with difficulty: "No. Except that he may have tried to fight off the thieves."

"There's no sense to it," McGee declared. "Somebody takes a lot of pains to get in here. When they're in, they pass up a lot of valuable stuff and take two necklaces that don't add up to so much. They kill Homer Stratton and hide him in a suit of armor, then somebody else comes in, pulls over the armor, yells bloody-murder, and beats it. I ask you, does it make sense?"

"It's horrible!" Stratton exclaimed. "To think that for an hour—more than an hour—while the store was open—

Uncle Homer's dead body was in that suit of armor and nobody knew it—"

"Put there to keep it hid and throw us off the track—maybe," McGee answered. "Sit tight, young fella. Where is he?"

"In there," Stratton said, indicating the door. "The medical examiner and fingerprint expert are there, too, with Baxter. I couldn't stand it."

McGee stepped to the door which connected with the house beyond. He paused, looked over his shoulder, and asked: "Got any idea who that girl was, Stratton?"

"No!" Stratton said.

McGee went through. In the library, a richly furnished room, he found Baxter, Nelson and Stone, together with all that remained of Homer Stratton. The body of the jeweler had been removed from the suit of mail, which was piled in a glittering heap on the floor. McGee took a look at Homer Stratton's bashed head and sighed.

"What's the dope?" he asked.

"No fingerprints anywhere," said Stone. "No way of telling who put him in that tin can."

"Dead from two blows on the head," said Dr. Nelson. "But that's not all. He was disabled, before he was killed, by a shot of tear gas. The smell's still on his clothes. He got a dose of the stuff, and then he was clubbed with the butt of an automatic. Thin skull—it finished him off quick."

"There's this, Show-Me," Baxter spoke up. "Coat pocket."

McGee took from Baxter a crumpled sheet of paper. He read it rapidly:

My dear Stratton:

This will introduce you to Mr. Henry Ritch, an assistant
of mine....

"Somebody named Littlefield arranging to borrow the
Monson collection, looks like," McGee observed. "Little-
field—that's the name of the curator of the International
Art Museum, isn't it?"

"Right," said Baxter. "As for Ritch, I don't know. He's
not in the phone book or the directory."

"Uh-huh," said McGee. "I'll take this, Box-Car. Littlefield. I'm going up to see that guy...."

MR. JOE SMITZ was not a man who enjoyed social standing. He was a collector of refuse and garbage, and offici-
ated in the rear end of a Municipal Sanitary Department
truck. It was shortly after eleven o'clock when Mr. Smitz's
vehicle drew to a stop near the front of the house of the
late Homer Stratton.

Mr. Smitz lugged into his cart the can which stood on
the curb there. He dumped out its contents, whistling
blithely. He replaced the can and then, as was his wont,
poked hopefully among the débris. Rarely did Mr. Smitz
find anything justifying his eternal hopes. But this morning an unusual item struck his eye.

It was a small, flat box covered with red leather stamped
in gold. Mr. Smitz opened it and ceased whistling. He
gasped; his dirty fingers picked from the plush lining a
string of beads which glittered pinkly in the sunlight. Mr.
Smitz said "Geez!"

Quickly he turned his back so his driver couldn't see, and
looked at the necklace anew. Avarice rose within him. This

thing looked good. Mamie'd be tickled to death if he gave
it to her... But maybe that wouldn't be so good. There was
something wrong, a nice string of beads like this showing
up among rumpled newspapers and sandwich wrappings.
Mr. Smitz's avarice ebbed low as prudence ascended.

"Wait a minute, Ike!" he howled to his driver.

Mr. Smitz thought it would be better not to take a
chance; and, anyway, there'd be a reward. He walked back
to the entrance of Homer Stratton, Inc., and went in.
Scarcely harmonizing with the surroundings, he stepped
to the counter and asked the clerk behind it:

"Know anything about this?"

"My word!" said the clerk. "Where'd you get this? You'd
better come with me!"

The clerk was Edward Dean, the oldest employee of
Homer Stratton, Inc. He was aged, but he could move fast,
and he negotiated the stairway to the balcony at a fast clip.
He placed the box in the desk in front of Arthur Strat-
ton, and Stratton started. Just at that moment Show-Me
McGee emerged through the connecting door.

"It's the pearl necklace that was stolen last night, Mr.
Stratton!" Edward Dean gasped.

"I found it in the garbage can," spoke up Mr. Smitz.

Show-Me McGee heard and came closer. He peered at
the necklace. He listened to the exciting talk that passed
between Stratton and Dean, and looked at the blank, dirty
face of Joe Smitz.

"This—this," said Stratton, rising, and speaking to Mr.
Smitz, "is rather valuable. We're grateful for its return,
although it was fully covered by insurance. Thank you very
much. Here's something for you."

Twenty dollars to Mr. Smitz was, indeed, something! He grabbed the bill, hurried down the stairs, and away. McGee peered keenly at Stratton; and he looked a bit angry.

"What the hell!" he blurted. "Some guy commits murder so he can rob a vault, grabs himself a pearl necklace, and then throws it into a rubbish can as soon as he gets out of the place! This business makes less and less sense!"

"I don't understand!" Stratton blurted. "The only thing missing now is the Monson gold necklace—worth at most five hundred. Why would any thief throw away the more valuable of his two pieces of loot and keep one that isn't worth one-fortieth as much?"

"Let *me* ask *you* questions!" McGee snapped. "Why should any crook throw that pearl necklace away after once getting his mitts on it?"

"Why—why—he may have known that it would be extremely difficult to dispose of. This is a fine necklace. All the pearls in it are registered. It could easily have been traced."

"Then why was it taken in the first place?" McGee demanded. "If this crook was smart enough to know that, why did he cart it out of the place?"

"Perhaps he thought he could break the necklace and use the pearls separately, then decided it was too much of a risk, and wasn't worth it. The separate pearls are worth a good deal less than the whole matched string."

"NOPE. I DON'T believe it," Show-Me McGee stated. "Maybe he took the necklace as a blind. He must've come here to kill Homer Stratton, and pulled a robbery to throw us off the track. Who'd do that? Some enemy of your uncle's—"

"Uncle Homer had no enemies," Arthur Stratton asserted. "How could he have? He's scarcely gone out of this store and his house in years. He's conducted his business on the highest plane. I don't know of a single person who might even wish to kill him, let alone do it."

"I'll take you at your word, but it's against my principles," McGee answered impatiently. "But if he wasn't killed for revenge, or hate, and if robbery wasn't the reason—what the devil could be the motive? What about that Monson necklace?"

"The Monson collection," Arthur Stratton explained, "does not belong to this store. It is the property of Mrs. Herbert Monson, whose husband died a month ago. He made the collection. It is all period jewelry, intrinsically not worth very much, but the pieces have some value as antiques. Mrs. Monson left it with us to sell. She stipulated that only the whole collection could be bought—no separate pieces. "There's not much of a market. The only one interested person so far has been Thomas Littlefield of the—"

"Ah?" interrupted McGee. "Littlefield?"

"Of the International Art Museum. He thought he might add it to the museum's collection of period jewelry, but he was doubtful. A few days ago he was in, and looked it over, and asked if he might borrow it for a day or so, so that he could inspect the different pieces and take photographs for the benefit of the museum trustees."

"Littlefield, hmm?" asked McGee. "I'm going to see him. You sit tight here, young man."

He turned toward the stairs. At the top step he hesitated.

"You say you don't know anything about the girl who came in here and pulled the suit of armor over and yelped?"

"I know nothing about her," Stratton answered.

Show-Me McGee trod down the stairs, plodded toward the corner entrance.

At the counter near the door he spied Edward Dean, who had returned to his station. McGee leaned across the counter. "Were you right here near the door when that girl went running out of here? Did you happen to see her?"

"Yes. Yes," said Dean.

" 'D you ever seen her before?"

"Yes," said Dean.

"What! You had! Why the devil didn't you say so?"

"Because nobody asked me," Dean answered promptly. "I have seen that young lady in the store many times. I think she is a friend of Mr. Arthur Stratton."

"A friend—!" McGee stared hard and cynically discounted what he was hearing by nine-tenths. "What makes you think so?"

"Months ago she used to come in and ask for Mr. Arthur Stratton, and he would come down and talk with her. Once or twice she went up to the balcony to see him. But lately she's come in without seeing him."

"Know her name?"

"No, sir."

"Well," said Show-Me McGee irrelevantly, "you can't believe what you see in the newspapers."

He walked out the door, hesitated, fingered the purse in his pocket thoughtfully. He turned again, walked through the store, climbed the stairs, and trod toward the desk of

Arthur Stratton. As Stratton looked up, McGee leveled a stern finger at him.

"Young man," he said, "even if you were telling the truth I probably wouldn't believe you, but I happen to know you've been lying to me. You said you didn't know the young lady who screamed. You do know her. No—don't try to explain because I wouldn't trust a word you said. Only, think it over. That's all I'm saying to you right now—think it over."

Arthur Stratton turned white and swallowed hard as Show-Me McGee turned his back to him and trod down the stairs. His haggard eyes followed McGee all the way out the corner entrance....

McGEE DEPOSITED HIS two hundred pounds on the brake-pedal of his roadster, squeezed himself out, and crossed the street to the entrance of the rambling white stone structure that was the International Museum of Art. He wanted to see Mr. Thomas Littlefield. In three minutes he was entering Mr. Littlefield's office.

The curator of the museum was a dusty, well-dressed, bald-headed man who inquired what he could do for Mr. McGee.

McGee handed him the letter found on Horner Stratton's body. Tell me about that," he asked.

Littlefield's eyebrows arched as he regarded the letter. "I can't tell you much about it," he declared, "except that I didn't write it."

"You didn't!" McGee exclaimed. "Isn't that your signature?"

"It looks like my signature, but it's forged."

McGee promptly drew his notebook from his pocket

and spread it open. He produced his fountain pen and unscrewed the cap. He placed both objects on the desk in front of Littlefield.

"Show me," he said.

Littlefield wrote his signature on the page. McGee studied it, compared it with that affixed to the letter.

"You're right—but they're similar," he decided. "I don't believe the signature on this letter is real—but I don't believe it's a fake, either. Suppose it's a forgery. Somebody was trying to get at the Monson collection, using your name. Who would it be?"

"I really couldn't say," Littlefield answered.

"You could," McGee asserted, "if you knew that Stratton's was robbed last night, and Stratton was killed by somebody who stole a necklace from the Monson collection—one worth less than five hundred bucks."

Littlefield started. "Good Lord! You don't mean old Homer Stratton is dead! You say killed—"

"Listen," McGee interrupted. "If this letter is a fake, it was framed by somebody who knew you'd made tentative arrangements to borrow the Monson collection. Who might that be?"

Littlefield looked blank. Suddenly his face lighted. "Jeffers knew of it!"

"Who's Jeffers?"

"I made the acquaintance of the gentleman recently—Mr. Milton Jeffers. He came here, inspected the exhibits, then asked to see me. We discussed various matters pertaining to our collections. He was a charming man. We—"

"Got on famously together. Uh-huh," said McGee.

"Why, yes. He took me to lunch several times, and we discussed Renaissance art and—other matters. When I dropped into Homer Stratton's to look at the Monson collection, he was with me. He heard me arrange to borrow the collection—but I haven't done so. Other than those in the store—say, Mr. Arthur Stratton—he's the only person who—"

"What," asked McGee, "is Mr. Jeffers' address? Got it?"

"Yes." Littlefield thumbed through his wallet, drew out a card. "One-seventy-one Parkleigh Avenue, Apartment 6D."

"Thank you," said McGee, "very much."

He went out, without further ado, scribbling in his notebook. He mumbled to himself:

"Some guys are certainly gullible!"

3

ROUGH ON MCGEE

NUMBER 171 PARKLEIGH Avenue was a wealthy-looking apartment building on a corner. McGee breezed past the telephone operator in the gold-and-gilt lobby, wedged himself into a tiny elevator, and got off at the sixth floor. His knuckles rapped upon a door labeled *D.*

A quick step answered. The door inched open and an eye peered out.

"Did you get—"

The question broke off suddenly as the eye centered on McGee's face. McGee kneed at the door, forced it open another inch. He stepped inside, closed the door behind him, and gazed distastefully upon the man who had answered his call.

The object of his scrutiny was small, lean, hard-faced, and shifty-eyed.

"Heard the news?" McGee asked.

"What? What news? What do you want here?" The questions came rapidly and uneasily from the shifty-eyed one.

"Stratton's was held up last night, and old Homer Stratton went cold from a rap on the conk," said McGee. "Or," he added thoughtfully, "maybe that isn't news to you."

The hard face grew harder. "What do you mean?"

"I mean, Mr. Jeffers," said McGee, "that this is just routine questioning on my part. I don't like it. But I've got to get it over with. I won't believe much of what you tell me, but go ahead and talk. This bird Littlefield, for instance. Just to show how much you can depend on what you hear, he said you were a charming gentleman."

The shifty eyes grew narrow. "What kind of a line is that you're pulling? Talk? I'm not going to talk. I don't know a damn thing—"

"Let's you and I," said McGee, "take a little spin. It's a nice drive down to Headquarters."

The other man's hard face grew shades whiter. He appeared to hesitate. His right hand stole to his vest pocket and removed what appeared to be a fountain pen.

"All right, I'll go with you," he said. "Mind if I leave a note?"

"Not at all," McGee agreed.

The hard-faced man turned to move beyond the table. His step took him closer to McGee and as he moved he appeared to try to unscrew the cap of the thing which appeared to be a pen. The end of it swung up, pointed at McGee's face.

Hiss!

McGee gasped, choked. Suddenly his eyes were red-hot, bursting with pain. He felt the stinging onslaught of the tear gas deep in his lungs. He leaped aside, sputtering, grabbing at the holster in his hip-pocket.

"You dirty—" he choked.

The other man leaped back swiftly, scowling, his face screwed into an expression of savage brutality. His move toward his gun was as fast as McGee's. It flashed up as McGee stumbled aside, made a pass at his face, futilely trying to wipe the torture from his eyes.

A terrific blow landed on McGee's chin, driving him backward. He grunted, flung his arms out. He felt his right hand grasped and instantly jerked at the trigger of his automatic. Too late! It was gone from his hand before he realized it. He forced his eyes open, saw through streaming tears, blearily, the other man leveling a gun directly at him....

Stinging agony forced McGee's eyes shut as he flung himself aside.

Instantly he heard the flat roar of the gun in the room. Terrific power struck his head. He sobbed, dropped to his knees, clung blindly to a chair. For one instant the black world whirled around him.

The next instant McGee was out cold....

DISTINCTLY SURPRISED, McGEE felt himself coming around. He hadn't expected that. During that last instant of consciousness he had considered himself duly shot through the head and murdered. Skeptically he raised himself, opened his blurred eyes, and looked around.

The philosophy of his father, old Dan McGee, patrolman, now dead and gone, bless his soul, never seemed sounder than at this moment: to believe only half of what one saw. For, stretched out on the carpet, on the other side of the table, lay the man who had attempted to kill McGee!

McGee struggled up, threw open four windows, blundered into the adjoining bathroom, dashed a towel in cold water, and bathed his smarting eyes. Able to see a bit more clearly, he came back and looked again. It was true. The man on the floor lay face up, his shirt bloody—dead.

McGee lifted the automatic from the hand of the man on the floor and smelled of it. The tear gas had done things to his smelling apparatus, but he was able to discover that the gun was clean! It hadn't been fired!

"Lord, a guy can't believe nothing!" McGee moaned.

He pushed his head out the window for a gulp of fresh air. Six stories below, near the corner, he saw something blue. It was a flat-foot. McGee knew the man who had this beat. He bawled:

"Owens! Mike Owens!"

Owens peered up.

"Come up here, Owens!" McGee yelled.

As Owens trotted around the corner, toward the entrance of the apartment building, McGee turned back. He deposited the would-be murderer's gun on the table, hurried back to the bathroom, and observed the reflection of the top of his head. There was an egg-sized lump over his left ear, and the skin was only partly broken.

"No bullet did that," McGee decided, "but I don't know."

He surveyed the living room of the apartment quickly. What had happened? Evidently plenty had happened while he was blinded and stunned by the tear gas!

"Somebody came in the door while I was staggering around," he said aloud. "Whoever it was, he clipped Jeffers with a bullet, then slugged me. That might be what happened, but there's no way of telling."

One thing McGee could not doubt: that the man on the floor was dead. He was, *quite*. And another truth was that it was this man who had killed old Homer Stratton.

The use of the tear gun, preliminary to more deadly attack, indicated that.

"Unless," thought McGee, always skeptical, "there's more'n one guy working one of those damn fountain pen guns that shoot tear gas!"

He grabbed the telephone and, when the operator below answered, snapped questions:

"I'm McGee, from Headquarters. Got that? I'm in 6D. Understand? Who came up here a little while ago—just a—well, I don't know how long ago it was, but somebody came up to this apartment. Who was it?"

"Why," said the voice, "Mr. Jeffers."

"No, no! I mean the bird that came in and went right out again."

"Mr. Jeffers."

McGee sighed. "Let's get this straight. Who rents this apartment?"

"Mr. Jeffers."

"And who was the guy who came in and went out right away?"

"Mr. Jeffers."

"I don't mean the little guy with the ugly face and the shifty eyes and the brown suit! I mean—"

"Mr. Jeffers," came inexorably. "The gentleman in the brown suit is Mr. Ritch."

"Ritch!" McGee shouted the name. "Mr. Ritch was already up here, was he, then Mr. Jeffers came in and went out again, quick?"

"Yes, sir."

McGee felt dizzy. "Did this Mr. Jeffers happen to tell

you where the hell he was going when he went out so quick?"

"No, sir."

Knuckles were hammering on the door. The spring-lock had caught and fastened it. McGee hooked the receiver, strode to the door, opened it. Patrolman Owens strode in, stopped, blinked.

"Somebody havin' a party?" he asked.

"Tea," said McGee sourly. "Listen, Owens. You're taking charge here. Call the medical examiner, the fingerprint expert, the governor and the militia if you need 'em. I'm in a hurry. I'll give 'em all the dope afterwards."

Owens was staring in the general direction of McGee's necktie.

"Say! What's—"

"Yes, and keep everybody else out of here!" McGee snapped.

He strode out the door. A minute later he had crammed himself behind the wheel of his roadster. His eyes and nose still felt raw, and they were dripping. He slammed the car into gear and whizzed off toward the downtown section.

When he bumped to a stop beside the huge store of Homer Stratton, Inc., Patrolman Morrissey was sauntering by. Morrissey stopped, stared at McGee and grinned.

"Hello, Show-Me," he said. "Say, what's—"

"I wouldn't believe it if you swore to it," McGee snapped, and strode by.

He lumbered through the corner entrance of the big store, and stopped at the first counter, where Edward Dean was officiating. Leaning across, he asked:

"Where's Stratton—the young one?"

"In the house, Mr. McGee," said Dean. "My goodness, may I ask why—what's—"

McGee strode on without listening. "Can't a guy look funny without being asked to give reasons?" he asked himself as he climbed the stairs. He looked back, and found half a dozen clerks staring after him in bewilderment. On the balcony, finding the connecting door open, he sighed—and went through.

Arthur Stratton was in the library. The body of Homer Stratton had been removed. The pile of armor had also been taken away. Stratton came quickly from a desk in the corner as McGee entered.

"Listen! You know anything about a bird named Jeffers?"

"Jeffers? No. McGee, what in Heaven's name—"

"I'm asking! Do you remember Jeffers as the man who came in with Littlefield when Littlefield talked with Homer Stratton about borrowing the Monson collection?"

"Yes—I remember now. There was a man by that name. I scarcely noticed him. McGee, do you realize—"

"Me, I don't realize anything unless I can help it!" McGee snapped, wiping his wet nose. "What did this bird Jeffers look like? Tell me anything and everything about him you—"

"Wait!" Arthur Stratton exclaimed desperately. "Do you realize what you've got around your neck? Look at it! Do you mean to tell me you don't know—"

McGee blinked. He turned quickly, toward a mirror that hung over the fireplace. He stared at his reflection, and for the first time grasped the reason for the bewildered questions.

Hanging daintily around his neck was a delicately fili-greed necklace of gold!

"McGee," Stratton declared breathlessly, "that's the necklace that was stolen from the Monson collection!"

4

"IT MOVED!"

McGEE TOOK IT off. He gulped and stared at it. The strands of *filigrane* trailed daintily across his calloused palm. A moan came from him.

"I didn't know that thing was there!" he blurted. "Lord, I must've been wearing it all the way from Jeffers' apartment!"

"Jeffers' apartment? What're you talking about, McGee?"

McGee blew his nose violently. "I know what happened—maybe. There's a crook named Jeffers. He found out, through Littlefield, about the Monson collection. He had a guy helping him named Ritch. Last night Ritch came here with a letter to which Littlefield's name was forged, arranging to borrow the Monson collection.

"Maybe the idea was to get the whole collection and walk off with it like that. But something happened. Homer Stratton got suspicious. Then Ritch gave him a dose of tear gas from a fountain pen gun, and slugged him. Ritch went into the vault and took the pearl necklace and the Monson necklace. As you say, he could've helped himself to a hundred grand worth of stones, but he didn't—he took just those two things."

"We've checked up twice. There's nothing else missing," Stratton echoed.

"Okay. Then Ritch hid Homer Stratton in the suit of armor, to delay the discovery of the body. Ritch went out, and promptly chucked the pearl necklace into the rubbish can. He must've done that to make it look like a big robbery, and because he knew he'd be caught if he tried to market the beads.

"Well, I found Ritch over at Jeffers' apartment—traced it through Littlefield. When I tried to grab Ritch, he sprayed me full of sputter-gas and started to shoot me. Just at that time Jeffers popped in the door—I guess it was Jeffers. Then what did Jeffers do? He shot Ritch instead of me! And then, while I was knocked out, he put this necklace on me! The more I see of this case the less sense it makes!"

"He must've got rid of the necklace because it was getting too hot for him," Stratton suggested rapidly.

"That doesn't make sense, either. It's just as hot for Jeffers without the necklace as with it—he's implicated in one murder and directly guilty of a second. He could've kept the necklace if he'd wanted it—but he didn't want it. He got away clean, and a sweet job I've got of finding him!"

Stratton was fingering the necklace. "Look here!" he exclaimed. "I'm going to have this examined. I'm not closely acquainted with it, but Dean is. I'll call him."

As Stratton hurried out the door, McGee picked up the telephone. He was asking for Headquarters when Stratton returned, followed by Dean. They had met on the stairs. Cupping the transmitter, McGee turned to listen.

"Look at this, Edward," Stratton urged. "We didn't inspect the Monson collection minutely because it isn't ours, but you're more familiar with it than I am. This *is* the necklace, isn't it?"

McGee's connection came through. "Sullivan," he said. "Got that taxi-driver yet? Well, when you locate him, haul him in and phone me. Listen. We got something on the teletype the other day about a slick jewel crook who was seen moving this way. How about it?"

Sullivan answered: "Right, Show-Me. The name is Jejer—Max Jejer. Slick as a whistle, wanted in New York. Thought to be in this region, hiding out."

"Jejer! That's close enough! Got prints on him, and all the rest? Anybody seen him here in town? No? Well, he's here, baby—he's here!"

McGee hung up and faced Stratton and Dean. The old jeweler raised his head from a close inspection of the necklace and looked very puzzled.

"No, Mr. Stratton," he said gravely. "This is not the Monson necklace."

"What!" barked McGee.

"It isn't?" echoed Stratton.

"No, sir. It's a very good replica. You know, the Monson necklace was one of the least valuable pieces in the collection. Even its value as an antique wasn't exceptional. Its period was indefinite—the work defective. But this—Mr. Stratton, this is an excellent piece of work. The gold in it is finer than in the original! The stones in it are genuine diamonds, but in the Monson necklace they were only crystal!"

McGee took a deep breath.

"The fact of the matter is, Mr. Stratton," said Dean, "that

this necklace is far more valuable than the one that was stolen from us!"

McGee stared at Stratton. Stratton stared at Dean. Dean stared at them both.

"Take it down, Edward," said the young man, "and put it in the safe."

"Yes, sir. The store is just closing, sir, and I'll just have time."

McGee's gaze followed the old jeweler out the door. He sank into a chair and mopped at his eyes.

"This is a lulu!" he said. "A crook makes a careful plan to rob, kills a man doing it, passes up the most valuable pieces within reach and picks out two comparatively low-priced necklaces—then chucks one in a rubbish can and replaces the other with a duplicate that costs more than the original! My old father was right. A man can't trust anything!"

THE ESTABLISHMENT OF Homer Stratton, Inc., was closing for the night. The corner entrance was shut and bolted; the steel shutters on the windows were lowered; the clerks were busily storing trays of valuables in the vault. Swiftly the items were checked over, and the employees began leaving through a rear entrance.

Edward Dean lingered, making sure of the last details. Arthur Stratton descended the stairway, closed the vault, and spun the combination. From a rear corner, where he sat, Detective Sergeant James Baxter watched the proceedings with interest. At last he rose, climbed the stairs, stepped through the connecting door, and found Show-Me McGee slumped in a chair in the library.

"Listen, Box-Car!" McGee said, sitting up suddenly. "This thing is pretty well doped out. The bird we want is

an international jewel thief named Max Jejer. He's engi-
neered this little deal, but he's skipped. We've got to find
him. That's our job—to find Jejer.

"Robbery and two murders—that's what we want him
for. He's been living in an apartment over at 171 Parkleigh
Avenue, but he'll never go back there any more. He's either
skipped out of town by now, or he's hiding—we've got to
smoke him out. You and I, Box-Car, are beating it down
to Headquarters for a look at that bird's record."

Arthur Stratton returned through the connecting door,
followed by Edward Dean.

"Come on, Box-Car," McGee said, rising. "We're on
our way."

He turned away with Baxter, then paused and regarded
young Stratton with a skeptical eye.

"You thought it over?" he inquired.

"What? What do you mean?"

"I mean about that young lady who came in here this
morning and pulled over the suit of armor and howled. You
coming clean about her?"

"I don't know what you're talking about!" Arthur Stratton exclaimed. "I'm sure—"

Suddenly, cutting through Stratton's words, a shrill,
sharp scream sounded!

It was a woman's cry of terror. It came through the
connecting door, echoing from the walls of the huge store
beyond. McGee stopped in his tracks; Stratton's face
flashed white. They stood an instant, paralyzed.

"This place gets full of screeching sopranos!" McGee
blurted angrily.

He hurried to the connecting door, through it, and

crossed the balcony. He stared downward over the railing as Baxter and Stratton pressed close beside him. Below, in the rear corner, was a young woman.

She was standing rigid. The suit of armor had been reassembled and replaced on its pedestal; and she was staring up at it, paralyzed with fear. McGee made a startled, guttural exclamation which reached her.

McGee bounded down the stairs, hurried along the aisle toward her. She retreated against the partition wall, one hand raised to her throat. Her face was white, her coloring vivid. Pretty—very pretty, and dark. As McGee barged toward her she turned, stared again at the suit of armor and gasped:

"It moved!"

She made no attempt to get away. McGee, Baxter, Stratton and Dean surrounded her, and she stared from one to another of them. McGee skeptically raised the visor of the steel helmet of the form on the platform, and satisfied himself that the shell was empty. He turned back as Stratton asked the girl angrily:

"How'd you get in here?"

"The store is closed, you know!" echoed Dean.

THE GIRL STAMMERED: "I—I'm sorry. I didn't know. I—I was in there and—just came out."

She indicated the door behind her. McGee glared at it and asked:

"What is that place, anyway, that howling women come out of?"

"The rest room," said Dean.

Stratton turned on the old employee. "How does it

happen she was left in there, Edward? You know we always make sure no one is in the rest room before we close up."

"We did," Dean declared. "I didn't look, of course, Mr. Stratton. I don't peek into ladies' rest rooms. Miss Wilson did, though—I saw her. She went in, and came out, and told me no one was in there."

"Miss Wilson," Stratton explained quickly to McGee, "is a stenographer. It's her job to see that the rest room is empty before we close for the night. But if she said it *was* empty"—Stratton peered at the dark young woman— "how could you've been in there?"

"I don't know!" the girl exclaimed. "She must have been mistaken. I came in late—I was looking at dinner rings. I felt faint, so I went in there for a few minutes. I didn't realize that the store was closing. When I came out, and found the place shut tight, and everybody gone—why, naturally, I was a bit frightened. I was standing here, wondering what to do, when all at once—I saw that suit of armor move!"

"So you screamed," McGee added wryly. "I don't know that I believe you, but it sounds likely."

"Really—that's all," the girl said. "I'm terribly sorry. I didn't realize—"

McGee lifted the hip-plate of the armor and took another squint into the interior.

It was empty, right enough. No dead body hidden inside this time.

"Kind of funny it would happen like that," he observed. "There's nothing in the papers yet—we've kept it quiet. Maybe that thing was just settling." He turned a keen eye upon Dean. "This isn't the same young lady who was in here this morning, is it?"

"Oh, no, sir," Dean answered. "The other young lady was a blonde."

"Well," said McGee wearily, "just as a matter of form, I'll take your name and address, miss. I guess it's all a mistake, and there's no need of holding you."

The dark young woman looked vastly relieved. "My name is Alice Dustin," she answered. "I live at Forty Emerald Avenue. I assure you—"

"Aw, that's all right," McGee said, scribbling in his notebook. "Sorry you were scared. I hope you're feeling all right now. Dean, show her the way out."

Dean seemed hesitant; Stratton was uncertain. McGee waved a dismissing hand, and stepped back. Dean meekly signaled the young woman to follow him and led her to the employee's entrance, in the rear of the store. McGee watched while the door opened and the young woman went out.

Instantly he grasped Baxter's arm.

"Move, Box-Car! Beat it around and go out the house door! Keep that woman in sight—follow her! Don't let her give you the slip! And when you've found out where she's going, phone Headquarters!"

Baxter jerked. "Show-Me, you're slick! I thought you were letting her off pretty easy!"

He whirled on his heel, dashed up the stairway, and disappeared across the balcony through the connecting door. McGee stepped quickly to one of the shuttered windows and applied his eyes to a crack.

Through the slit he saw the dark young woman hurrying to a sedan parked near the corner. She slipped behind the wheel, started it, slid away from the curb. As she spurted the car around the corner, McGee shifted his eyes back and picked up Baxter. Baxter was hailing a taxi. The next moment the taxi was wheeling into the main street after the sedan.

McGee had a head for numbers. He'd noted the license plate of the sedan before it disappeared. Turning, he trudged back to the desk beside the vault, and picked up the telephone.

"Sullivan!" he exclaimed. "Got the car list there? Look up right now X5-34-42... Okay, I'm waiting."

He waited.

Sullivan's information came: "Registered in the name of Jeffers, Show-Me. Milton Jeffers, 171 Parkleigh Avenue."

"I," said McGee with gratification in his voice, "am much obliged!"

He lowered the phone, smiling.

"I thought so! This is all tying up. That young woman who gave her name as Alice Dustin is connected with Jeffers, alias Jejer. He must've sent her here. She stayed in this store after it was closed, deliberately."

"But why?" Stratton demanded.

McGee didn't answer. He fixed a stern eye on Stratton. "I suppose," he said, "you don't know that one, either?"

"I never saw her before in my life!"

"Uh-huh. Well, I'm telling you again, Stratton—think it over. I'm in no hurry to make you talk, and I wouldn't believe you if you did talk. You're not going to slip away, either. I've got no reason to press you. It's all coming out. Only, as I said before—think it over!"

McGee turned toward the employee's entrance. Dean

opened the door for him, and he trudged out without a word.

5

McGEE, FROM MISSOURI

McGEE, REMEMBERING THAT he had had no lunch, trudged into a nearby restaurant and ordered food. He ate slowly, wearily, thoughtfully. When he paid his check he slipped into a telephone booth and called Headquarters.

"Sullivan," he said. "What's the dope from 171 Parkleigh?"

"Not much," Sullivan answered. "Stone found finger-prints all over the place that match with Jejer's. Jeffers is Jejer, all right. I've signaled all the call boxes and the prowl cars to look out for him, but there's nothing doing so far. Probably he hasn't skipped out of town; he's in hiding."

"How about the bird named Ritch?"

"He's Harry Reif, alias Henry Ritch, in the same racket. Dope from New York says he's pulled some jobs with Jejer. There's a woman tied up with it, too; she's been seen in Jejer's apartment. In fact, she's known there as Mrs. Jeffers. Name's Irma Decker, also wanted in New York."

"Dark? Pretty?" McGee asked.

"Right. Now about the taxi-driver you wanted, Show-Me. He's here now. Tells a straight story. Want the details?"

"I do," said McGee.

"He said he was waiting outside of Stratton's when this woman came hurrying out. Says he didn't know anything was wrong. She jumped in, and he drove away in a hurry because she said to. Then she discovered that she'd lost her purse, and didn't have any money, so she told him to drive her home. He did."

"Where's she live?"

"In an apartment at 56 Frost Street. I've been checking up on her. Her name's Jeane Nichols. Lives on the third floor, rear. The renting agent has her listed as secretary to the president of the McCord-Mason Company, and I've checked on that. Okay."

"Sounds funny," McGee observed. "That'll do for a starter. Better let the taxi-driver go and warn him about picking up women who run out of jewelry stores in a hell of a hurry. The trouble with most guys is that they believe too much."

McGee hung up. Pausing in the booth, he dragged the blue purse from his pocket, opened it, and extracted the little folded note. His eyes played speculatively on the phrase "I've got it" and on the initials, "AS." He noted "Meet me at seven, your place," and glanced at his watch. It was a little past six-thirty.

McGee left the booth and the restaurant and stepped outside to find it raining.

"You certainly can't believe these weather-prophets," he remarked to himself. "The paper said fair tonight."

He crossed the spattered street, wedged himself behind the wheel of his roadster, and started off. The retail section was almost empty now, and quiet. McGee turned corners, pulled into a through street, and kept straight. He decided to pay a call on Miss Jeane Nichols of 56 Frost Street.

IT WAS A modest apartment building, a walk-up affair. McGee left his roadster at the entrance, ducked through the downpour, and trudged up the stairs. At the door of the apartment on the third floor, rear, he knocked.

The knob turned, the door opened. A girl looked out, smiling; but her smile disappeared quickly when she beheld McGee, and she caught her breath. McGee tipped his dripping hat.

"I want to come in," he said. "I'm from Headquarters."

"Why—why, certainly," Miss Jeane Nichols answered.

McGee found himself in a small, attractively furnished, feminine room. It was the kind of a room an unmarried professional woman earning a good salary would live in. Jeane Nichols fitted into it harmoniously. She was blond, and pretty, and frightened.

"Do you usually go around, pulling suits of armor down on yourself?" McGee inquired quietly.

"Oh!" said Miss Jeane Nichols.

"Well, do you? When they contain the bodies of murdered men?"

"Oh, please!" the girl exclaimed. "I didn't know—really I didn't!"

"You certainly got out of there in a hell of a hurry," McGee commented. "It looks pretty suspicious to me. Maybe you were after that note?"

Jeane Nichols looked terrified. "I—I didn't realize— what was inside the suit of armor. The note was—"

"Forged," McGee said bluntly. "And by means of it I began running down Jejer. That's why you came after it, wasn't it? Before Stratton's body was found? To get that note back, because it could be traced."

The girl looked bewildered. "Forged? I—I don't understand!"

"You wouldn't," McGee said bluntly. "Well, that's the way it looks to me. First Jejer sent you to get the note, if you could, and you couldn't, because you pulled the armor down on you. Then he sent his other woman—Irma Decker. That right?"

"Irma Decker? I—I don't know anyone of that name! I don't know anyone named Jejer, either. I don't know what you're talking about!"

"That makes it tough," McGee said. "I was hoping you'd come across. Since you won't, then the only thing to do is to take you down to Headquarters and cool you off until you do talk. Better bring an umbrella with you—it's wet."

"You—you're taking me to Headquarters?"

"Well, not to any movie, anyway. Let's go." McGee was stolidly determined about it.

And the girl's terror increased. "But why?" she cried. "It was all so—I didn't dream—I was so frightened I acted on impulse! Don't—"

In the room a buzzer sounded. The girl grew quiet suddenly, staring toward the door. McGee quickly slipped out his watch—the fat time-piece bequeathed to him by Dan McGee—and glared at it. Seven o'clock exactly.

"I'll take it!" McGee said quickly.

He turned to the door, grasped the knob, opened it. A young man was waiting in the hallway; he began to hurry in, but, seeing McGee, stopped. "I thought so!" said McGee.

Jeane Nichols' caller was Arthur Stratton!

McGEE TUGGED AT Stratton's arm, and shut the door behind him. Stratton was startled, dismayed. He turned from McGee quickly and looked at the girl anxiously.

"Jeane! What's—"

"He says he's taking me to headquarters, Arthur!" the girl exclaimed.

"That's nonsense—sheer nonsense!" Stratton blurted. "McGee, you're making a sad mistake!"

"Yeah?" McGee said skeptically. "I admit I don't get this, but it looks to me like you and this young woman and Jejer are all mixed up together. What is it—a plan so you could rob your own uncle's store?"

"McGee," said Stratton grimly, "you are very near to being socked one on the nose. That's going too far! If I wanted to rob the store, why should I pick out two comparatively cheap necklaces, then throw one away and replace the other with a duplicate more valuable than the original?"

"Why should anybody, for that matter?" McGee asked.

Stratton faced McGee angrily. "Now, get this straight. I'll tell you the whole truth about the matter. I admit I lied to you about knowing Miss Nichols, but it was only to keep her out of this mess. She's perfectly innocent of any wrong-doing, and so am I—but as long as you've hunted her down, I'll explain."

"Make it good," McGee commented. "I'm not very gullible."

"Miss Nichols and I," Stratton resumed, "are engaged to be married. We've been planning it for months. She used to drop into the store to see me, on her way to work, and sometimes during the day she would call me up. Uncle

Homer got nasty about it. He expected me to think of nothing but business during business hours. He objected to Jeane's dropping in and phoning, and was so strict about it that I didn't even dare phone her."

"Well?"

"Well, we had to keep in touch with each other, didn't we? To make dates—to see each other? Certainly! What we did was simply to arrange a way of communicating with each other quickly. We left notes for each other in the suit of armor near the rest room door. I know that sounds silly to you—but it wasn't to us. It was the only way we could get in touch with each other during the day. Sometimes I would leave a note for Jeane under the hip-flap of the armor, and she would drop in and get it without anyone's knowing it. Sometimes she would leave notes for me there."

Jeane Nichols added desperately: "When I came in this morning it was only to get a note from Arthur. As I took it out of the flap of the armor, I saw something inside—a hand in the gauntlet. Naturally I was frightened. I screamed. And then, knowing that the excitement I was causing would get Arthur into trouble, I hurried out. It really was quite innocent."

"And when you asked me if I knew Jeane, McGee," Stratton emphasized, "I said I didn't, because I knew what had happened, and I wanted to keep her out of it."

"Uh-huh," said McGee skeptically. He removed the blue purse from his pocket, opened it, and extracted the folded note. "But what does this mean? 'I've got it'? That refers to the stuff stolen from the safe?"

"It certainly does not!" Stratton denied.

"Then what—"

"It refers to a marriage license!"

McGee blinked. He looked at the girl and saw that her cheeks were very red. He eyed Stratton and said: "You've got to show me!"

Stratton promptly removed his wallet and from the wallet removed a folded bit of paper. He thrust it into McGee's hands. McGee read it troubledly. It was a marriage license, all right. Issued to Arthur Stratton and Jeane Nichols.

"We were tired of waiting, tired of Uncle Homer's watching us all the time," Stratton declared. "We decided to quit this thing of sneaking notes to each other. I left the note for Jeane saying I had the license, and that I'd meet her here. I didn't want to waste another minute—we planned to be married tonight!"

"Arthur!" sobbed Jeane.

She came to Stratton; he enclosed her in his arms. They clung to each other tightly; he raised her chin, and kissed her full on the lips. It was a long kiss.

"Well—" said McGee doubtfully.

The kiss continued.

"I guess—" said McGee.

They still kissed.

"The way I look at it—"

McGee gave up. He turned to the window, and looked out into the rain. Presently, when he heard a movement behind him, he turned and tossed the blue purse on the table, note and all.

"I've been shown," he said.

"NOW" ARTHUR STRATTON demanded, "is it necessary to take Jeane to Headquarters?"

"Naw," McGee answered. "There's some things I don't believe, but I've got to believe you two kids love each other, and you're on the square. Only, it leaves me in a hell of a hole."

"But, Arthur, dear," Jeane said, "now we must wait. We can't be married now—so soon after—"

"I know it," Stratton answered, glumly.

McGee sighed. "I'd like to use your telephone," he said.

Again he called Headquarters. As he stood at the phone, he heard eloquent sounds behind him and discreetly kept his back turned. Even so, he found it a bit hard to keep his mind on business.

"Sullivan," he said. "Any report—"

"Baxter just phoned!" Sullivan answered. "He reports he followed the girl 'way out in the country. There's a cabin in the woods on a side-road three miles from Benjamin's Crossing. She went there in the sedan—and there was a man in the place when she arrived. Baxter's waiting for you now."

"And I bet he's plenty wet!" McGee answered with a snap. "I'm on my way, Sully! Get a couple of our best furnished rooms all set for guests!"

6

INITIALED "N-J"

McGEE SAID "SORRY!" to Stratton and the girl, and hurried out the door. He thumped down the stairs, ducked through the rain, wheezed into his roadster, and spurted away from the curb. Benjamin's Crossing was an intersection of roads a good five miles from the center of town. He stepped on the gas.

Ten minutes later he whizzed past the crossing, with the rain sluicing across his windshield and spraying under the top. He slowed, searching for the side-road which branched off a short distance away. He turned onto it, a muddy, rough stretch leading into the blackness of the woods.

He took it easy, wary that the lights of his approaching car might warn those in the cabin ahead. He was scarcely two miles from the Crossing when he saw a movement in his headlights—a form duck out of the bushes. It was a very moist Baxter. Baxter waved his arms; McGee splashed to a stop.

The detective sergeant hopped to the running-board, breathing hard.

"Steady, Show-Me! They're in the cabin about a mile

ahead! Better get off the road right away and we'll make it the rest of the way on foot!"

"Okay," McGee said grimly. "The papers said 'fair tonight.' Let that be a lesson to you!"

A few rods farther on he drew the car to the muddy side of the road, clicked off the lights and the ignition. Baxter lowered himself; McGee opened the door.

"The girl came all the way out here in the sedan, Show-Me," Baxter said. "She didn't catch on that I was following her—I kept out of sight. I watched my chance and slipped up close. I could hear her talking with somebody inside."

"See him?"

"No. Couldn't take the chance. Sounded like they weren't so keen about things. I heard the man say, 'You sure they weren't pulling a fast one, letting you go?' And the girl said, 'I had to get out of sight, anyway, didn't I? You let me in for a hell of a mess.'"

"Meaning she damn near got caught," McGee nodded.

"Then the man said, 'Irma, I didn't know they'd found Stratton till after I sent you. You were already on your way when I went to the apartment and found Reif there with the dick. It was too late then to stop you.' And she said, 'Well, if we don't get out of here *toot sweet* we'll have the whole police force stopping us.'"

"You did well, Box-Car," McGee observed. "That pins it on 'em. The girl is Irma Decker and the man is Max Jejer. They've pulled this whole business, but damn if I can see yet why."

Rain was dripping off the end of Baxter's nose. "It may be clear to you, but damn if I see it," he said.

McGee got out of the car. "Lead the way," he ordered, and began trudging after Baxter through the black woods. Rain poured down from the evergreens, drenching them.

"It's this way, Box-Car," McGee explained. "Jejer planned to grab the Monson collection by using a note with Little-field's name forged to it. Ritch, or Reif, his sidekick, was to grab the stuff and in doing it Reif killed Homer Strat-ton. He hid the body in the armor, but he forgot about the forged note in Stratton's pocket."

They were following a trail, their shoes sloshing in the softened earth.

"Then Jejer planned it so his girl friend, this brunette, Irma Decker, would go back to the store, hide in it when it closed, and try to get the note out of Stratton's pocket. They didn't know the body'd already been found. The Decker woman was already on her way, the move all planned out, when I barged into Jejer's apartment on Parkleigh.

"Why Jejer killed Reif I don't know, but he did, and he put that duplicate necklace around my neck. He beat it, apparently out here to this cabin. It was too late then to call the Decker woman off. She got into the store, but she must have caught a bad case of the jitters when she found Stratton's body gone out of the armor. You know the rest."

They were moving into the open now, and the down-pour was heavier. McGee was already soaked to the skin.

"I got this much," Baxter said. "Reif stole the pearls to throw us off on a false scent, and chucked 'em into the refuse can so they wouldn't be caught with 'em, and because the pearls were too hard to dispose of and too easy to trace. But I can't figure why he picked out that one Monson necklace when he might have had the whole collection."

"And then replaced it with a necklace worth lots more," McGee sighed. "I'd hate to think what a gullible detective would be making of this case. It certainly pays to be skeptical."

Baxter quickly gripped McGee's arm. "It's ahead, Show-Me. How'll we tackle 'em?"

"Follow me," said McGee....

THEY DUCKED THROUGH an arm of the wood, and into a hollow. Abruptly the cabin loomed before them. It was a log shack, centered in a clearing. Its windows were curtained, but a few chinks of light shone between the logs. McGee paused, looked over the layout, then began creeping closer.

Baxter kept at his heels. The rustle of the rain drowned out possible sounds of their movements. A few yards from the cabin, McGee paused, eying the sedan which was sitting beside it. He signaled Baxter to wait, then eased over to the car.

Baxter watched him curiously. McGee quietly raised the hood of the sedan and did something with his hands. As silently, he replaced the hood and drifted back to Baxter.

"Let's take a listen," he whispered.

They stepped carefully to the side of the cabin. Rain dripped from the roof and upon their shoulders as they hunched, ears turned to a chink between the logs. There were movements inside—someone walking across the floor.

Presently a man's voice said impatiently: "For God's sake, sit down!"

"Max, I can't sit still!" came the woman's answer. "If the cop I barged into, in Stratton's, hadn't been so thick-headed, I'd have been in the jug now. You're taking too many chances!"

McGee said "Huh!" very quietly.

"You can thank Reif for the trouble we're in," the man inside retorted. "He forgot the note, didn't he?—the chump! That's what blew up the works. If he hadn't done that, we could have gone through as I planned it first— kept the original and returned the duplicate necklace, and probably nobody would have noticed it. Not until after we were out of here, anyway."

"You didn't have to kill him, did you?"

"No?" the man asked quietly. "I should have let him kill the dick, should I? Sure! It would have brought every flat-foot in town down on us! That's the kind of a sap Reif was—fool enough to bump off a cop. Besides that, he would have turned on the phonograph. We're a damned sight safer with Reif out of it—and now we split only two ways. You pull yourself together, Irma."

There was a pause. The woman's light footfalls crossed the board floor.

"Yes? And if you bump me off, you won't have to split at all."

"What're you talking about? You know I'm crazy about you. Cut it out—you're upset, that's all. I tell you we're all right."

" 'All right'! All this over that two-for-a-nickel necklace. When you had the chance why didn't you grab some real stuff?"

"Because we're hiding out, that's why. Because we had a chance to switch the necklace without anybody knowing I was behind it. Because this thing is worth a damned sight more than anything else in the store!"

"That?" the woman asked. "It's nothing but plain gold with pieces of crystal in it. You're out of your head!"

"Listen!" The man's command was sibilant. "This is one of the biggest things we've ever grabbed! Nobody but me knows how much it's worth. Littlefield didn't know, and Stratton didn't know, and the Monsons didn't know. I spotted it quick—give me credit!"

"Yeah?" the woman asked slowly.

"LOOK HERE." THE man's voice was excited now. "Look through this magnifying glass. See the back side of the clasp, there? See those marks that look like scratches? They're not scratches—it's engraving, worn away, partly. See it?"

"Yes."

"What does it look like?"

"It's—it's two initials," the woman answered. "The first is an N. Then there's a J. Well, what's that?"

"That," said the man, "is what makes this necklace worth a hundred grand anywhere!"

"A hundred—"

"Those two initials," the man continued excitedly, "mean *Napoleon to Josephine!*"

Silence again, inside. McGee turned his dripping head toward Baxter. Baxter looked up at him with widened eyes....

The man's voice continued inside: "It was a gift from the Emperor Napoleon to Josephine, Irma! That's what the inscription means! I saw it the first time I picked the necklace up in Stratton's, when I was with Littlefield. Nobody's noticed it before that! God, you've got to have eyes in this business—and I used 'em!"

"Max! Is that true?"

"True as gospel! Without those initials, this necklace wouldn't be worth our looking at, even as an antique. With 'em—we're in clover! Did you think I was a fool, making the duplicate out of better gold and using real diamonds? I didn't have anything else to use, and I didn't care. I can sell this necklace anywhere, in America or Europe, for more money than you ever dreamed existed!"

McGee drew away from the wall, tapping Baxter's arm. Back a few yards, he put his mouth close to Baxter's wet ear.

"Take the back door. I'll go to the front. Soon as I'm there, start knocking and order 'em to open up. They'll probably come in my direction."

Baxter nodded, drifted away through the downpour. McGee waited until he was sure Baxter was in place, then skirted around to the front door of the cabin. He drew his automatic, stood at one side, and waited.

Suddenly loud knocking sounded from the rear.

"Open up!" Baxter called.

Within the cabin there was a sudden silence. McGee stood taut, still waiting, his gun leveled. There was no movement inside.

The knock came again.

"Open 'er up!"

Suddenly a blast of shots shook the cabin. Three, four times a gun roared within the four log walls, so swiftly that the reports seemed one explosion. McGee jerked, backed away a bit, tightened the grip on his gun.

"Max!" the woman exclaimed.

"I told you it was a trap! They followed you!"

McGee was listening anxiously toward the rear of the shack. He heard a splashy sound, a dull moan. Then Baxter's voice came, a strained mumbling of words:

"Got me—Show-Me—"

McGee's massive jaws clamped hard. He slipped off the porch, slid along the side of the cabin, paused. Dimly he could see Baxter on the ground, writhing, trying to crawl away. He turned swiftly, jumped back to the front of the cabin.

Reaching out one long arm, he hammered his knuckles on the rough wood of the door.

"Come on out!" he commanded.

Again there was silence inside. McGee stooped, peered through a narrow chink between the logs. He could see little—the dark form of a man standing in the center of the cabin, the woman beside him. They must have guns, but he couldn't see that much. He raised, hammered his fist on the boards savagely.

"You're coming out!"

Jejer's voice answered harshly: "If you want us, come in and get us!"

McGee squared his shoulders, stepped away. As he did so, a gun inside the shack spoke again; a splinter of wood flew out into the rain, and a spot of light appeared in the board. McGee rushed, flung up a leg, brought his two hundred pounds against the door in a stiff-kneed thrust.

The door shook, crackled, and held.

Another bullet splintered through, and tore at the skirt of McGee's coat.

"If you come in here you'll arrive dead!" the voice inside threatened.

"You've got to show me!" McGee gasped.

He lurched forward again. This time his shoulder met the door, his full weight crashed against it. Boards cracked, and the latch inside burst.

McGee stumbled in, propelled by his momentum. His gun was leveled, his eyes shifting right and left quickly. The center of the room was empty now. The man and the woman were on both sides of the door.

McGee whirled as the guns crashed at him.

Red lightning flashed before his eyes. Thunder rocked through his brain as he spun about, losing balance. He felt himself falling and fired once, blindly. His bullet drilled into the floor. His body thumped against the boards, sprawled out, motionless.

He'd got it in the head....

McGEE ROLLED OVER, slowly, a mass of pain. He blinked his eyes, and stared up at the crude ceiling. His head was bursting; the salt taste of blood was in his mouth. He lay panting, while the rain drummed on the roof, while tom-toms beat against his brain.

Suddenly he tried to get up. He felt his movements impeded, and fell back. Struggling to a sitting position, he looked at himself. There was a great wet spot on the floor where he had fallen, with a blending of red in it. Rain was still dripping off him.

And his hands and ankles were cuffed together... McGee blinked at them, until he realized one pair of handcuffs was his own, the other Baxter's.

He moaned and rubbed his head. His fingers came

away wet, his head throbbed more brutally. The bullet had furrowed above his temple, making an ugly gash. Over half an inch, and it would have bore through... "Box-Car!" McGee shouted.

The sound of his own voice made the pain worse. Sitting there, waiting for his strength to come back, he tried to figure how much time had elapsed. There was no way of being sure. Of course, Jejer and the Decker woman were gone....

The cabin was out in the middle of nowhere. The nearest phone must be more than a mile away. McGee thought of that, then forgot it. Very carefully he doubled up, balanced himself, and straightened. He came to his feet, swaying....

The link of the handcuffs on his ankles was so short he couldn't step an inch. McGee tried it, tottered, regained his balance, and decided to hop. He hopped; and the jolt brought a new pain into his head that made him groan. But he hopped again....

Once he looked around the cabin. On a table, in the corner, was a litter of strange apparatus. McGee made out a Bunsen burner, pliers, tweezers, a thing that might be a jeweler's blowtorch, and a few scraps of metal that gleamed in the light and looked valuable. Jejer's tools, with which he had fashioned the duplicate of the Napoleonic necklace. He'd gone off in a hurry.

McGee hopped again, wriggling to keep his balance, and reached the front door. It was still raining hard. He hopped, hopped, around the side of the cabin. Grimly he noted that the sedan was still in its place.

"I still know a trick or two!" he gasped.

Hop. Hop. Hop. McGee reached the rear corner of the

shack. There was Baxter, still lying in the rain. McGee bent over him, shook him. Baxter gave no response.

McGee stooped, gripped Baxter's arms. He pulled, hopped, pulled again, hopped again, toward the sedan. It drained his strength and made his head drum, but he kept it up. The distance to the door of the sedan was only a few yards, but it seemed miles. At last McGee paused, leaning against the car, puffing....

He wrenched the rear door open. Bracing himself, stooping, he dragged Baxter up. It was a strenuous, painful job, getting Baxter into the car. He managed it at last and paused, exhausted.

Slamming the rear door, he hopped to the front fender. Twisting himself, he managed to thrust his hands into his right side pocket. The cloth was wet; it clung maddeningly. With an angry push and pull McGee reached the thing he wanted, and jerked his hands out. Small coins scattered into the mud when his hands came free.

Bending, he loosened the catches of the sedan hood. He raised it, and fitted the thing he had taken from his pocket into the distributor housing of the ignition system. He replaced the cap, lowered the hood, and sighed.

Hopping again, he reached the driver's door, jerked it open, and pulled himself into the seat. He noted that the floor mat was wet with prints.

Jejer had tried to start the sedan and failed—because McGee had taken the precaution of removing the distributor arm.

McGee twisted on the ignition—the key was there, abandoned as Jejer had left the car. The starter ground; the motor whirred. McGee found it difficult to work the pedals with his cuffed feet, but it could be done. He gripped the wheel at its lower edge and twisted the car toward the road.

With the lights on, he followed the ruts. He was in no hurry. Breathing hard, squinting with pain, he kept driving. The rain was lessening now, but the ground was soft... Presently McGee braked, and brought the sedan to a stop.

His own roadster sat at the side of the road. He wriggled out, hopped toward it. Looking in, he saw wet marks again on the floor mat. Someone had been in that car, trying to start it, but McGee had the key. With an effort, he wrenched the seat cushion loose, probed into a wad of waste, and brought out a thirty-eight revolver.

Hop. Hop. Hop. McGee jumped back to the car, grimacing with the torture in his head. With the revolver in his lap, he started up again. The ruts helped guide him; he took it slowly. Still he was in no hurry. He knew the side road carried no traffic worth thinking about, and the road to Benjamin's Crossing scarcely more....

Almost at the crossing, he leaned forward, peering. In the glare of his headlights he saw movements. A man and a woman were hurrying along the side of the road, each carrying a small case. They paused, looked at the sedan, signaled with their arms.

"Glad to oblige," McGee mumbled.

The man and woman stopped, waiting. Jejer! Irma Decker! Wet as fish, both of them, their faces white and desperate. McGee smiled grimly, drew the car to a stop beside them. He wrenched open the door, swung his feet out, and leveled the gun.

"Up!" he said.

Jejer jerked to a stop, staring. The woman had hurried to

the sedan first; she paused, and a little cry came through her lips. McGee hopped down. He saw Jejer reaching in his pocket for a gun.

McGee fired once, swiftly. The bullet ripped through the sleeve of Jejer's coat. Quickly McGee whirled, flung his arms up and down again. When they came down they were around the woman. He twisted about, pinioning her arms at her sides, and leveled the gun at Jejer.

"Get in, mister," he said. "Drop your purse, lady. I don't want you pulling any toy automatics on me!"

Jejer's face was livid in the glare of the headlamps. The shock and nearness of McGee's bullet had stunned him. McGee kept his thirty-eight straight out.

"Drop the artillery in the mud, Jejer. Get in at the wheel. You, lady, skip around to the other side and don't try to pick up your purse when I let you go, else I'll be tempted to put a bullet in you. Got it?"

Jejer's gun splashed into a puddle. Released, Irma Decker hurried to the far side of the car and ducked in, gasping. Keeping his revolver on them, McGee hopped into the rear seat, stumbled over Baxter's legs, sprawled on the cushion.

"What'd you do with the keys to these cuffs—lose 'em?" he asked. And when no answer came, he observed: "Well, they'll saw 'em off of me without much trouble, at Head-quarters. That's where we're heading."

McGee settled back comfortably as the car started. "Not too fast," he warned. "All I have to do is plug you, you know."

Jejer was grimly silent. Irma Decker was crying silently. McGee braced himself, gun still levelled.

"You can't believe what you read in the papers," he observed. "The papers this morning said, 'Fair.'"

WITH HIS HEAD bandaged, and moving a bit slowly, Show-Me McGee trod up the stairs to the third floor of the apartment house, and knocked at the door in the rear. Jeane Nichols opened it. He strode in, smiling, nodding to Arthur Stratton, who rose to shake his hand.

"Well," he said, "I guess it's all right. It's all in the papers, and you've read 'em. I just came here to say I'm sorry I was a bit hard on you. I guess maybe I owe you a little wedding present, don't I?"

"Forget it, McGee," Stratton smiled.

"The way I figure it," McGee answered, "is that I owe you two a lot. If Miss Nichols hadn't seen the body in the armor and got scared, probably nobody would've known it was there until later. Then the Decker woman would've been able to get the forged note back, and where would I've been? That was the only real clue I had to work on. So I figure I owe—"

"If you feel like that about it, McGee, I'll ask a favor of you," Stratton suggested. "Jeane and I are going to be married soon and—well, I want you to be my best man."

McGee looked startled. "Best man? Me? Why, I don't know anything about getting married!" Then he grinned, and flapped his hat against his thigh. "Why, sure. Proud to. I don't know what to do, though. You'll have to show me."

THE KILLER IN THE TOWER

*Eighty Stories Above the Street, When Death
Struck Like a Bolt From the Blue, Detective
"Show-Me" McGee Was Mysteriously
Trapped in the Observation Tower*

IT WAS JUST another day in the observation tower of the great Cloud Building, a humdrum and routine day, until the crack of a shot brought blood and turmoil into it.

It was mid-morning, and twenty-odd persons were circling the perimeter of the glassed-in observation platform. The crystal air and the bright sunshine had induced them to spend seventy-five cents each for a view of the city from the rearing spire of the skyscraper.

Beneath the eyes of the sight-seers the metropolis sparkled and hummed. In the chasms of the streets toy-like automobiles crept along, tiny streetcars crawled, and microscopic people drifted in herds. Flags fluttered below, over exposed roofs and nestling penthouses. Viewed from the height of eighty stories, the city seemed like a bed of cubistic crustaceans.

From time to time more observers stepped onto the dizzy platform from the elevators which appeared and disappeared noiselessly behind the bronze doors of the central shaft. Behind the counter of an alcove, a red-headed girl was selling colored post-cards and souvenir booklets. Near one window an artist was sitting at an easel, touching his brush to an oil-painting of the spreading panorama.

The artist was a handsome young man, and his work was attracting almost as much attention as the view. Silently they watched him dab color here and there, and compared his picture with the reality. He was oblivious of them, absorbed in his work. No one suspected, of course, that very shortly he would become oblivious of everything in this world.

The door of the center elevator slid open quietly, and its solitary passenger stepped onto the platform. He walked straight toward the artist, and reached toward his hip-pocket. The artist was bending over, wriggling a brush at a lower corner of his painting, as the newcomer drew a gun.

The gun spat flame. It was leveled within a foot of the artist's middle as the murderer pulled the trigger. The artist had looked up at that instant. With a bullet in his vitals, he fell toward the man who had shot him.

The cracking report of the weapon startled every person on the platform. Those on that side of the elevator shafts turned to see the artist toppling and the painting falling off his overturned easel. The murderer sprang away as the young man struck the floor. Quick steps took him toward the elevator which still stood open at the platform level.

He stepped into the cage and thrust his gun against the ribs of the uniformed operator.

"Go down!" he commanded.

The terrified elevator boy obeyed the command.

DETECTIVE LIEUTENANT McGEE, who was called "Show-Me" because he hailed from Missouri and consisted of two hundred pounds of hard-boiled skepticism, heard the shot.

Until that moment he had been busy pointing out landmarks to the little old lady who stood beside him. The little

As the bronze doors slid open, McGee thrust his
gun forward and said: "Stick up your hands!"

old lady was Miss Amanda McGee, and she was the detective's aunt. It was the first time she had come to the big
city since the construction of the famed Cloud Building,
and she had insisted that her hulking nephew show her
the sights from the observation tower.

Aunt Amanda was in many ways a remarkable woman.
Over seventy now, she had several times in her girlhood
crossed the American deserts in a covered wagon, seeking with her husband, now dead, new frontiers. She was
hearty and hale and her eyes had a gleam. To her the slight
infirmities of her age were merely trifling inconveniences.
Aunt Amanda's bright mind would stand for no nonsense,
and as for living and getting about, she could very well take
care of herself.

"Over there," McGee was telling her, "is the new gas works—"

"Where the tough gangs hang out," Aunt Amanda nodded.

"Yes, that's so—the toughest gangs in the city. That spire over there is the Paracraft Theater, the biggest—"

"That's where the theatrical booking agent was murdered last week, isn't it?" Aunt Amanda asked. "I remember reading all about it. He was stabbed four times, and his throat was cut. It was very bloody."

McGee cast an amazed eye at the little old lady and agreed that it had been very bloody. "That," he said, pointing again to a spread of green, "is Westmore Park. Since you seem to be interested in such things, I might say that within the past month three bodies have been found in the shrubbery over there, tied up with gunnysacks and riddled—"

"Three?" asked Amanda. "I'm sure it was four, John. Three men and a woman, and she didn't have a stitch of clothes on, and she'd been choked and beaten and—goodness!"

Aunt Amanda's exclamation mixed with the sharp report of a revolver that cracked through the rarefied air of the platform.

Show-Me McGee spun on his heel. He abandoned the little old lady and broke into a run, reaching for his service gat. The shot had come from the other side of the tower.

As he swung past the corner, he saw the artist sprawled on the floor, the painting lying beside the overturned easel.

"He went into an elevator! I saw him run into the elevator!" It was the red-headed girl, behind the counter in the alcove, who screeched the information at McGee.

"The middle one!" someone else gasped.

McGee sprang toward it. The bronze door of the shaft was already shut. The indicator above it was already recording the downward passage of the car. McGee punched the button frantically. He hammered on the door and shouted. The needle of the indicator continued to turn downward—but suddenly it stopped.

McGee began punching every signal button in sight. Fast work was imperative. The stopping of the elevator into which the murderer had gone indicated that the killer might be getting out at some lower floor to hunt cover in the busy vastness of the skyscraper. If McGee could reach the ground level first, he might stand a chance of making a grab before the murderer escaped from the building. But to do that McGee needed an elevator, and needed it badly.

No car appeared in response to McGee's frantic ringing. The clocks above the bronze doors showed that no cars were even coming up. In a moment McGee noticed that, also, no cars were going down. The hand of every indicator was motionless.

McGee swung around to the postcard counter. There was a telephone. He grabbed it up and called a special police number. Swiftly the connection was made.

"Sullivan!" he snapped. "Guy killed in the tower of the Cloud Building. The murderer's beating it. Signal the nearest squad cars to close in around the building. Tell the boys that nobody's to be let out—nobody."

McGee dashed back to the elevators. The clock hands above the doors had not moved. He punched the buttons again, puzzled, fuming at the delay. He was still punching

them when the telephone on the post-card counter clattered.

The trembling red-headed girl listened through the
instrument, put it down, and began to make a quavering
announcement to the horrified sightseers.

"L-ladies and gentlemen. The elevator s-service is
temporarily suspended. The cars will be running again in
a m-moment. Please don't be alarmed." She was exceedingly alarmed herself.

McGee strode to her. "What's that? The elevators are
on the blink?"

"Yes, sir. A fuse or something blew out. Every elevator
in the building is out of order. B-but they'll get 'em fixed
right away."

McGee hurried back to the bronze doors. The middle
elevator, he'd been told, was the one the killer had taken.
The indicator of that car was poised halfway between two
numerals. As he realized the meaning of that, McGee's
eyes gleamed with triumph.

It meant that the killer's car was hanging between levels
in the dizzy heights of the tower—caught between floors!
McGEE COULDN'T HAVE asked for a better break, and
he quickly took advantage of it. He shot questions at the
girl behind the counter. He learned that the elevators were
equipped with telephones, a separate system centering in
a master switchboard. The telephone on the counter could
not be connected with any of them, however, because it was
an entirely different hook-up. Still, the car into which the
murderer had fled could be reached indirectly through the
Business Manager's office.

McGee got to work. "Now get this, and don't waste

time asking questions," he said gruffly when the Business Manager's switchboard answered. "Police business—a killing here in the tower. Phone the operator of the center tower elevator and tell him not to move his car until ordered. If the power comes back on before he's told to move, he's to pretend it's still off. Got it? Gi' me your boss."

A man who identified himself as the Business Manager of the Cloud Building spoke over the line. McGee told him the facts succinctly and demanded further information concerning the elevators.

"The fuse-boxes for the elevators are on the fifty-second floor," he was told. "Electricians are on their way up now to repair the damage—they're going by way of the stairs. None of the cars are moving now, but it won't be long before—"

"But people can get out by the stairs, can't they?" McGee snapped. "Get somebody into the lobby and close all the doors. Nobody's going to leave this building until I say the word.

"There's a murderer somewhere inside this skyscraper, and we can't let him get away!"

As he put the phone down he heard the faint wail of a siren far below. Through the windows he could see, in the street, two tiny cars speeding toward the base of the Cloud Building. Police whistles were shrilling and traffic was stopped to make way for them. They were the radio cars, already on the job, rushing to barricade the doors.

McGee turned away, sighed, and found Aunt Amanda at his shoulder.

"Keep hold of yourself, now," he reassured her. "Don't go to pieces. It's all right—a dead man can't hurt you."

The little old lady's eyes were shining, and she was aflutter with excitement.

"Of course he can't hurt me, John. I don't have to keep hold of myself. I'm not going to pieces. I'm perfectly able to take care of myself. I've always wanted to see a real murder, and now I have."

McGee blinked in amazement.

"Don't you mind me at all, John," Aunt Amanda said. "You go right ahead and catch the murderer!"

She was cooler than any of the twenty-odd others on the observation platform. Two women had fainted and were being doused with ice-water and fanned. Another was clinging to her husband and babbling. A small boy was howling at the top of his lusty lungs. Somebody was hammering at an elevator door and shouting crazily to be let out. The others were huddled in groups by the rail, paralyzed with terror. Aunt Amanda alone seemed to be enjoying herself.

McGee walked to the dead man grimly and made a rapid examination. Seeing the red-headed girl staring at him behind the counter, he strode to her, and asked questions. McGee hated this question-asking routine, but it was necessary. Fortunately, the girl was able to give him some information.

The name of the dead man was Arthur Killerand. He had been painting a series of views from the tower, and had been at work daily for several weeks. He had spent the summer in his home town of Allenburg, Ohio, and had started the work immediately upon his return to the city. It seemed also that he was newly married; at least he had spoken of "my wife." The redhead had struck up a casual acquaintance with him; she thought he was a nice man, and was horrified at what had happened.

McGee used the telephone again. "Sullivan," he said, "get onto long distance—Allenburg, Ohio. Find out all you can about Arthur Killerand, an artist. Get it quick, and phone me back."

"It—it's terrible," the red-head exclaimed as McGee put the instrument down. "This was the last painting he was going to do, and he was just finishing it. I saw him putting his signature on it just as that man got out of the elevator and pulled the gun."

Hysterics still prevailed on the platform. McGee bawled at the sightseers, snapped at them, and showed them his badge. He told them to quiet down, and they did.

"Now," he demanded, "some of you saw the bird who did this killing. What did he look like?"

"He was a big man, with broad shoulders and big feet," the red-head volunteered. "He was wearing a black suit and a gray hat and—"

"No—that isn't true!" one of the men exclaimed. "He was only average size, and kind of skinny. His suit was gray, a pepper and salt—it was his hat that was black."

"Why, I saw him!" the red-head protested.

"I saw him myself," the man answered indignantly. "I was standing right in back of that artist when it happened."

One of the women spoke up. "Why, you're both wrong!" she ejaculated. "I saw him distinctly. I saw him run away and get into the middle elevator. He was wearing a brown suit, and a straw hat. I noticed the straw hat because it's so late in the season. And he had a mustache—a little mustache that—"

"He *didn't* have a mustache," another of the sightseers interrupted. "I know, because he ran right past me to get to the elevator. I got a good look at his face. He was clean-shaven. There's no mistake about that."

One of the other women pinched her lips firmly and strode straight to McGee.

"Mr. Detective, they don't know what they're talking about," she insisted. "I saw the whole thing. I was standing right *there* and I saw every bit of it. He was a middle-aged man, and he had long sideburns. He wasn't wearing any hat at all—he was bareheaded. His suit was a blue-serge, and he was short—shorter than I am—and—"

McGee let out a bellow. "That's enough!" he roared. "He was a tall, thin, heavy-set, short man, with a felt and a straw hat on his bare head, and he was wearing four different suits! For the love of Heaven! Pity me trying to identify a murderer with that description. Good lord, a man can't believe anything—not even an eye-witness!"

AUNT AMANDA, IGNORING all this, had stepped quietly toward the murdered man. He lay twisted on his back. His oil-painting was face up beside him, on top of the collapsed easel. Aunt Amanda seemed to be less interested in the corpse than in the painting.

"That's not bad," she said to herself, studying it. "Not at all bad."

McGee strode to her and took her arm firmly. "Aunt Amanda, you be careful of yourself. I've got enough trouble on my hands without you fainting."

Aunt Amanda straightened indignantly. "Indeed! John McGee, I'm not going to faint. You forget, young man, that I've set broken legs, and saved a man from dying of snake-bite, and brought babies into the world, and what's more, I saw your Uncle Timothy's leg cut off with an ax because gangrene had set in, and I never batted an eye. Faint, indeed!"

Aunt Amanda must have touched the dead man, for she paused to wipe a fleck of blood from her finger tips with her handkerchief.

"What's more, John," she said sternly, "if you'll take a look at this young man's clothes, and then at the painting, you'll see that—"

The clattering of the telephone sounded with nerve-jarring shrillness. McGee grabbed it up.

"Sullivan talking, Show-Me," came a voice from Headquarters. "I called the newspaper at Allenburg and got the dope. Killerand spent the summer there. Made a scandal. When he left, a woman went with him—a Mrs. Phelps. She's young and pretty, and she just upped and run off with this romantic artist. Her husband runs a department store, and about a week ago he left town.

"The talk going around is that he went out to get the man who stole his wife. She was a flighty, selfish woman, and he was hot-headed as hell. Mistreated her, I guess, but from what I could gather, this artist wouldn't have given her a much better break. He loves 'em and leaves 'em flat. So it's dollars to doughnuts Phelps followed the pair to town with the idea of putting a bullet into Killerand. And he just simply did it."

"Thought it would be something like that. A crime of passion. That means this Phelps will be a dangerous customer if we can ever single him out of this building full of people. Any description of him, Sully?"

"Hair half gray, average size, five feet eight, fair skin, doesn't wear glasses, brown eyes, and a long, narrow scar in front of the left temple. Picture coming by phone. Boy, they're eating this up out there!"

McGee filed that description in his memory. He was putting the phone down when it rang again.

"Detective McGee?" It was the business manager of the Cloud Building again. "The elevators will resume service in a moment. People have been using the stairs, and there's a tremendous crowd in the lobby. The congestion is terrific. The police at the doors are holding everybody in. Is that necessary? Can't you let those I know go out?"

"Let out the ones you know personally, and that's all," McGee conceded. "Absolutely nobody else."

"What about the elevator that—"

"Telephone the operator and tell him to shoot that car back up to the tower the instant the current goes back on."

"Yes, sir. I—there! The current's on now. The cars are beginning to run!"

McGee moved fast. He slammed down the telephone, and whirled about to the array of bronze doors. He slipped his service revolver into his hand—and several of the women on the platform screeched. McGee ignored them, and watched the indicators above the doors.

Two of them began to move, showing that the cars were dropping downward. The one in the center remained stationary for a long moment. McGee's eyes never left it.

Then the hand on the clock quivered. It began to slide along the rim of the dial.

The cage into which the killer had run was coming up.

McGee stepped aside, revolver leveled, and watched the

pointer creep to the letters OP at the twelve o'clock position. The hand stopped. The bronze doors clicked. And
then they slid open.

McGee shoved his gun forward and commanded: "Stick
up your hands!"

A startled elevator boy threw his arms upward and
blanched. McGee brought up short, blinking.

For the car, aside from the gulping operator, was empty.

SHOW-ME McGEE MADE a violent noise. He looked
dazedly around the car and sheepishly lowered his gun.

"All right," he moaned to the operator. "Put your hands
down. I didn't mean you. How'd that bird get out of this
elevator?"

The boy gulped. "You m-mean the one that p-pointed
the gun at m-me and—"

"Yes! Where'd he go?"

"He made me stop at the seventy-eighth floor—two
stories down—and he got off. I started down again—to
report it—but just then the power went off and—"

"Where'd he go? Did you see that?"

"He ran along the corridor, and went around the bend,
and that's all I know."

Men and women were crowding to the door of the
elevator, eager to get away from the dead man and out of
the tower. McGee shoved them back angrily. He ordered
the elevator operator to close the inside grille, and when
that was done he bellowed at the trapped sightseers.

"You can't go yet. You're material witnesses, all of you.
You'll all have to go down to Headquarters. Stand back!"

There was more screeching and some cursing, which
McGee stolidly ignored. A glance at the indicator of the

next elevator told him a car was coming up rapidly. He hoped it was somebody from Headquarters to relieve him. It was. Detective Sergeant James Baxter stepped from the cage to McGee's side.

"The mob's yours, Box-Car," the big detective announced to him. "Keep 'em here until Maria's ready to cart 'em off. The red-head over there is included. Me, I've got a job on my hands."

He strode into the cage and commanded the operator to take him to the ground floor without a stop. The grille was just closing when a slight old lady wriggled her way in. It was Aunt Amanda, and she was even more excited than before.

"The murderer's loose in the building, isn't he, John? Do you think he's got away? I hope not—I want to see you capture him. Do you know what to look for? He—"

"Aunt Amanda," McGee broke in, "don't you bother me, now. I've got to think."

He was thinking that he was in a tough spot. The Cloud Building, full of busy offices, was like a city within walls. Fully eighty thousand persons worked in it. Thousands more came and went every hour. It would be impossible to keep the doors barricaded for long. With the elevators working again, and the noon hour approaching, it would mean a turmoil beyond the capacity of the available police force to handle.

Besides, the building was a vastly intricate mechanism. It had three main entrances into the lobby on the ground floor, and no doubt others, for freight, for building employees. In the substructure there were three floors, like catacombs, spreading under the streets, in which the fugitive might try to lose himself.

Even if the skyscraper could be thoroughly searched while it maintained its ceaseless functioning, the procedure would take days.

All this Show-Me McGee thought of as the elevator whizzed downward, while Aunt Amanda watched him as though eager to speak.

One thing gave McGee heart. The central stairway, which zigzagged alongside the elevator shafts, led down through the core of the building to the street level, and no farther. The fugitive, if he followed them, would be forced into the lobby. Even if he hid on one of the floors along the way—seventy-eight of them—he must sooner or later try to make his escape through one of the three main entrances.

The elevator car whooshed and bounced to a stop. The grille clicked open, and McGee found himself facing a mob. The lobby was crammed with people, shoulder to shoulder, front to back, as tightly as sardines in a can. They were clamoring to be let out. At the doors, uniformed men were barring their way.

An excited middle-aged man grasped McGee's arm and sputteringly identified himself as the business manager. What could he do? he wanted to know. What could he do? The lobby was already as full of people as it could get, and more were continually coming down. The crowd was getting ugly. If it began to stampede, people would get hurt. There were children in there, crying.

McGee barked orders.

"Stop the elevators until the lobby is cleared. Let the

women out the north door—but no men. Put yourself at
the south door, and let anybody go you know personally.
If you don't know 'em, don't let 'em out—send 'em over to
the west door. I'll be there."

McGee began shouldering himself through the crowd
as the building manager climbed onto an ash receiver near
the elevators and screechingly repeated the directions. The
crowd began to mill, and for a moment the confusion was
stifling. McGee fought his way to the west entrance, to
find two prowl-car men there.

"Okay—we've got to let 'em out," he gasped at them.
"We'll try to make it as fast as we can. Frisk everybody for
a gun. Take a look inside every briefcase and package. The
man we want is average weight, five feet eight, fair-skinned,
has brown eyes, hair half gray, doesn't wear glasses, and has
a narrow scar in front of the left temple, Now let 'em come."

AS McGEE WEDGED himself on the left side of the doorway, so as to be able to spot that scar, one of the prowl car
men called warningly: "The north door, madam. Ladies go
out the north door. You can't come through here."

"Indeed I can," declared Amanda McGee.

And she did. She wriggled past and stationed herself at
McGee's side. He eyed her anxiously.

"Look here, Aunt Amanda, this is apt to be dangerous.
The man we want is desperate. Somebody might get hurt.
You stay back, now, so—"

"Don't be silly, John!" said Aunt Amanda sternly. "I can
take care of myself. Don't you forget that once my husband
and I were surrounded by a band of Mexican guerrillas in
the Mojave Desert, and we fought our way out. I killed
two of the greasers myself, and I'm not afraid of anybody."

McGee couldn't argue with Aunt Amanda. Her firm will and the crush at the door made it impossible.

Men began crowding through the single section of the entrance which remained open. McGee stopped each of them, gave each a swift once-over, and let them pass on to a frisking at the hands of the two prowl-car men. Most of those who came out were business men, middle-aged and annoyed.

Others were messenger boys, clerks, salesmen. Into each of their faces McGee peered.

It required quick work, for the noon hour was close at hand, and another horde would be gathering in the lobby. Women were filing out of the north entrance, a few men were coming out of the south door. When the crowd became thinner, McGee shouted that the elevator service might be resumed.

All the while Aunt Amanda stood at McGee's shoulder and keenly scanned the men who emerged.

McGee's face took on a grim look as the number of men waiting to leave became fewer. Nobody so far had fitted the killer's description. Unless the murderer had somehow contrived to slip out unseen, he was still in the building.

All the women were out of the lobby now. No one else was leaving by the south door. McGee called the building manager, asked sharp questions, and learned that it was quite impossible that the killer could have escaped by any other door. There was no way, the manager explained, that the murderer could have reached any other exit. Being forced to use the stairs, or to wait for an elevator after the resumption of service, he must inevitably emerge into the lobby.

"I'll get that guy," McGee declared, "if I have to keep this up a month."

The searching went on, McGee passing innocents toward the squad-car cops for a final going-over. Only a score of men remained. Then a dozen. And then none at all, except for those who were stepping out of the elevators into the lobby.

"Looks like he's got away, Show-Me," one of the squad-car men opined.

"Not much!" McGee snapped. "He's still in there. And sometime he's got to come out."

McGee passed another man, inspected still another and passed him. The next stepped up and McGee resignedly wagged him on.

"John—that's him!"

Aunt Amanda clutched at McGee's arm as she said it. McGee stiffened and glanced down to see the little old lady's bright eyes shining excitedly. And then he turned to take a better look at the man he had just signalled through.

That man was of average build, and of about the right height, and his eyes were brown; but nothing else about him tallied. Under his derby his hair showed black. His skin was not fair, and he was wearing tortoise-shell eyeglasses.

"No, Aunt Amanda," McGee said. "You've made a mistake."

Aunt Amanda was trembling. "I haven't made a mistake. That's the man! That's the man who killed the artist!"

THE MAN STOOD quietly, looking at the little old lady. "Madam," he remarked, "I'm sorry, but I don't know what you're talking about."

"You do so!" Aunt Amanda insisted. "You killed that artist in the tower, I know you did!"

"Aunt Amanda," McGee said firmly, "you can't accuse a man like that. You didn't even see the man who killed the artist. He was out of sight in the elevator before I got there, even."

The man was smiling and moving away. The little old lady screeched. "Stop him! He did it, I tell you! He's a murderer! Look at his sleeve!"

A quick movement of the suspect was the first response to the old lady's cry. He raised his right arm and looked down at it. A gasp of dismay escaped him. Instantly he sprang away.

"Get him!" McGee bellowed.

He leaped after the suspect. The man cried out furiously as McGee's hand grabbed at his shoulder. He whirled and struck out, driving a fist into McGee's face. At the same time he jerked up his vest and from the hollow of his drawn-in stomach jerked a revolver that had been nestling behind his belt.

McGee howled and leaped aside. The gun blazed twice, swiftly. The bullets clicked against the marble front of the Cloud Building as McGee, crouching, leaped again. The man spun about and began to spurt away as McGee dived for his legs.

Another blasting shot echoed from the front of the building. McGee felt his man fall, spill on the sidewalk. He scrambled up, staring at a blot of red on the pavement, a limp hand stretched out, the revolver loosened from it. He realized then that the suspect had fired a bullet into his own head.

The prowl-car men were crowding about. Pedestrians were swarming. McGee snatched up the gun, turned the dead man face up. The derby hat had fallen off a head of hair which—obviously now, in the bright sunlight—was dyed. The skin, McGee saw, was stained to a darker than natural color by a pigment wash. The eyeglasses were broken, and in front of the suicide's left temple was a thin, long scar which the sidepiece of tortoise-shell had covered.

"Keep 'em back!" McGee howled as the crowd collected. "Get the wagon over here. He's the guy, all right!"

He could see that now. A jealousy-crazed husband who had sought revenge on his wife's lover. A hot-tempered vengeance-seeker willing to abandon his home, his business, the society he had known, for the sake of evening a score, and seeking a new life.

He might never have been found if Aunt Amanda—

The little old lady was crowding at McGee's side.

"I told you, John," she said grimly. "I told you he was the man."

"Yeah," McGee sighed. "So you did. Only, how the devil did you know? He fooled me. He didn't look anything like—"

"I kept my wits about me," Aunt Amanda answered pertly. "John, don't you remember the red-headed girl said the artist was just signing the painting when he was shot? His signature was down in the right hand corner.

"The easel was knocked over because one of the two men—the murderer or the artist—must have hit it.

"I looked for paint somewhere on the artist's clothes, but there wasn't any. Artists don't get paint on themselves anyway, and that proved he didn't knock the painting over when he fell. It was the other man who did it—the man who killed him. He knocked against the painting, and some of it came off on his sleeve. John, see right here?"

Aunt Amanda stooped, unfolded the suicide's sleeve, and pointed to an oily moistness on the fabric. It was black, and on the black were letters of crimson. Backwards they read:

Killer.

"It's part of the artist's signature," Aunt Amanda explained, "and it marked him like a brand."

McGee blinked and sighed again. He took the little old lady's arm.

"Aunt Amanda," he said sternly, "you're coming down to Headquarters with me."

"My goodness, what for? Are you arresting me?" she asked quickly. "Did I do something wrong?"

"You did everything right," McGee said. "I'm certainly not arresting you. I want to introduce you to the Chief. I want him to put you on the force!"

THE DEVIL'S DOZEN

Show–Me McGee Scowled Down At the Corpse and Said: "When a Dead Man Kills Another Dead Man, What's a Man Supposed to Think?" The Answer to That Grim Riddle Was As Strange As the Crime Itself

1

CRIME BY MINUTES

The huge banquet hall of the Claremore Hotel glittered and buzzed. Starched waiters bustled along the tables, clearing away the last of the coffee cups. Four hundred men in tuxedoes smoked and listened to the florid oratory of the Honorable James McGinnis. McGinnis aspired to become the city's next mayor. He was shouting about economizing, giving the people a square deal, and purging the city of crime.

"I promise you, gentlemen—and I promise it with all my heart and soul—that I will drive out of our fair homeland every last one of the human parasites which prey upon it!" he cried.

Deafening applause rocked the room. No one of the guests clapped his hands more approvingly than "Silk" Sprice, who was seated near the speakers' table, surrounded by his henchmen. Sprice was the city's Public Enemy Number One, and Numbers Two, Three, Four, *et seq.*, were his lieutenants. The lot of them were dubbed by the police "The Devil's Dozen."

Any racket was Sprice's meat, and he had waxed opulent and powerful. Recently, however, a great public drive against crime had been launched by a citizens' committee in cooperation with Headquarters, and Sprice had come upon hard times. It was rumored that The Devil's Dozen was looking for greener fields, that soon they would depart the city in search of richer pickings.

So Sprice—his presence at the banquet a grimly humorous gesture—applauded enthusiastically, and his henchmen shouted bravos.

In the doorway half a dozen plainclothes men loitered. They sent wary glances at Sprice's cohorts. If any of Sprice's

*The man on the stairs
screamed and came
spilling downward*

men should slip away from the banquet, an equal number of detectives would begin a bit of expert shadowing as part of their never-ceasing job of trying to get something on Sprice. But all The Devil's Dozen were present, and so far none of them had sneaked off.

And the speech-making went on flamboyantly.

Nine forty p.m.

In a house near the outskirts of the city there was quiet. The window shades were tightly drawn, and lights burned in only one room. In that room were four men, one of whom was seated laxly in a chair. The other three were alertly facing him.

"Wings" Williams was one of them. He was a keen-eyed, cunning breaker of laws, new to the city. Brains was his long suit. For years he had lived by his wits and lived excellently. Prior to his debut into crime as a society card-

McGee whirled against the wall as footsteps sounded behind him

shark, he had had a try at being an actor in New York. Tired of starving, he had undertaken to achieve luxury by relieving innocents, of their money. With all his illegal success, the theatre had never lost its lure for him. When on Broadway at the height of the season he loved to stroll backstage and hobnob with players in the wings. Hence his nickname.

The man standing at his elbow was "Twisty "Newton, so called because of a crooked nose. He was an ex-heavyweight and Williams' partner in crime.

The third of the group, facing the man in the chair, was Doc Reitz. The Doc was a trained physician who long ago had left the ranks of the ethical of his profession. Outlawed from respectable practice, he sold his skill to the underworld. He would supply drugs, remove bullets without reporting the wounds to the police, and perform illegal operations when asked. He had retained his skill, and made himself invaluable, to criminals.

"What's your name?" Doc Reitz asked the man in the chair.

The seated man looked tired; his eyes were vague; his face clouded with confusion. He made a visible effort to think, and answered Doc in a low tone:

"I don't know."

"Try to remember—what's your name?"

"I can't remember," the man said wearily.

This had been going on for an hour. To all questions concerning himself the man in the chair had answered negatively, unable to give any information concerning himself. He was perfectly sane, and not bodily ill, but some nervous connection in his brain had become broken.

Doc Reitz rose. As he stepped from the room he signalled Williams and Newton after him. They closed the door on the tired man in the chair and spoke in whispers.

"A clear case of amnesia—loss of memory," the Doc said.

Williams nodded. "He certainly is completely blank," he admitted.

"The condition is brought about by fatigue—overwork," Reitz went on. "Some intense nervous strain. Rest will probably bring him back to himself. Or some sudden, emotional shock. There's no telling for sure."

WILLIAMS NODDED, TOOK out his wallet, and passed a large bill to Reitz. He escorted the Doc to the front door and waited until the physician chugged off in a disreputable car. When Williams turned back to Newton his eyes were gleaming.

"God, what a break!" he exclaimed. "What a lucky break!"

Newton was slow-witted. "I don't get it," he said.

"We couldn't've wished for anything better. It plays right into our hands. You leave this to me, Twisty—I've got a plan. The slickest plan you ever heard of."

Williams reentered the room where the man was sitting in the chair. He drew another chair close and peered into the other man's tired eyes.

"I know your name," he said. "It's Henry Wilson."

The man frowned. "I don't—think so," he said.

"Yes, it is," Williams insisted; "Henry Wilson. That's your name. You remember now, don't you? You're Henry Wilson."

The man repeated vaguely: "Henry Wilson?"

"Yes. That's your name. It's the name you've been trying to remember. Isn't it? Now, what's your name?"

The man seemed about to speak, but he did not.

"Tell me your name."

"Henry—Henry Wilson."

"Sure! That's it!" Williams came to his feet excitedly. "Keep repeating to yourself—Henry Wilson. That's your name. Keep repeating it."

The lips of the man in the chair mumbled. Williams rose quietly and left the room with Newton. He glanced at his watch and ran quickly up the dark stairs to the second floor of the house, with his partner in crime at his heels.

"God, what a break!" he said again. "What a lucky break!"

Nine fifty-five.

Two miles away, in a modest residential section, another house was a-gleam with lights. Upstairs and down, every window glowed. But, except for one person, the house was empty.

Patricia Morrison moved about the sitting room nervously. She was distraught, afraid—which was why all the lights were burning. She found it an effort to keep the tears out of her deep blue eyes.

Every few seconds she glanced at the clock on the fire-place mantel, and each time she did so her anxiety increased.

She was twenty-two and pretty. She had prepared the supper which now sat cold on the kitchen stove. She had been waiting alone in the house for hours. As the minute-hand of the clock crept toward the hour of ten, she stepped quickly to the telephone and took it up. When she was about to lift the receiver, she heard a car stop at the curb.

Quick steps crossed the porch, and the front door swung open. A young man entered: he was just under thirty, and his face, too, pictured anxiety. He was David Washburn, an assistant automotive engineer in the great Luxcar plant, which manufactured low-priced automobiles. He came to the girl quickly and took her hands in his.

"You didn't find him?" she asked in a moan.

"I haven't located him, Patsy, but there's still a chance," he assured her breathlessly. "He left the shop this evening, right after he phoned you, but his car's still sitting in the parking space. He must have walked out for some reason, or else somebody picked him up—but that's only guess-work."

"Dave—we've got to call the police," Patricia declared wide-eyed.

"Not yet—there's one more chance," Washburn protested. "I've phoned Mattison and Leach and Kilgore—everybody—but they don't know where he is. I couldn't get Townland. I'm going over to his house and see if I can locate him. Wait until I get hold of Townland, Patsy."

"All right," the girl said resolutely. "I'll wait, Dave."

"Good girl! Townland doesn't answer the phone, and that may mean he's off somewhere with him. Not to the proving grounds, because I looked there—but somewhere else. Listen, darling. I'll phone you as soon as I've reached Townland's place and found out something."

"Hurry!" she said. "Oh, Dave, if something's happened to Dad—"

"Stiff upper lip, now," he told her. "Chin high. Good girl! I'll be right back."

Washburn hurried out the door. As the girl heard the motor of his car spin rushingly, the clock on the mantelpiece struck the hour of ten.

TEN O'CLOCK.

The grandfather clock was striking the hour in the living room of a house five miles from the center of the city. As it chimed, a knock sounded at the front entrance. Clarice, the maid, heard the summons and hurried to answer it.

She opened the door and looked out to see, standing in the dim light, a broad, stocky man whose hat shaded his face.

"Oh, good evening, Mr. Townland," she said.

"Good evening. Mr. Leach in?" the caller asked.

"Yes, he's in the sitting room. Step in, please, sir."

Clarice stepped through an adjoining door. Next to a table, on which a heavily shaded lamp was burning, Leonard Leach was sitting, reading a magazine. She announced that Mr. Townland was calling, and Leach rose to greet his visitor. Clarice retired upstairs as the caller stepped into the sitting room.

"Good evening, Townland," Leach said affably. "How are you?"

He extended his hand, but the other man did not offer to take it.

"I don't think you'll want to shake hands with me, Leach, when you learn why I've come," the caller said.

Leach looked confused and said: "What do you mean? What's the matter, Townland? Why *have* you come, then?"

"To kill you," said the other man.

Leach started to laugh. The statement was so unexpected, made in such a calm tone, that he could think of nothing else to do. Townland, like himself, was an automotive engineer at the Luxcar plant. They had worked shoulder to shoulder for years, and there had never been the slightest friction between them. Indeed, Leach considered himself one of Townland's closest friends. Under the circumstances his impulse to laugh was natural.

But his laugh broke off short when he glanced down. His caller's hand was raised now, but not for the purpose of grasping his. It was already grasping something—an automatic. The weapon glinted brightly in the lamplight, levelled at Leach's middle.

"What's the idea, anyway?" he started to ask, but the blast of the gun ended his words with a gasp.

Three times, swiftly, the automatic spat lead into Leach's body, at close range. Leach staggered back, clutching at his stomach. He half turned, as if to sit down, but before he could catch the arm of his chair, life went out of him. He fell with a thud.

The man who had brought death to Leonard Leach heard movements upstairs, and knew that the shots had startled Clarice. He crossed the room quickly, and picked up a telephone which was sitting on a taboret near the window. His hands were gloved, to eliminate the possibility of fingerprints, and he lifted the receiver without hesitation.

"I want a policeman," he said, according to the formula printed on the cover of the telephone directory.

The connection was made swiftly. A voice announced that Headquarters was on the other end of the line.

"Please connect me with the Chief," said the murderer.

"The Chief's not here. Who's calling? Something important?" the phone sergeant asked.

"Very important," declared the man in Leach's house. "A murder."

Unruffled, the sergeant said: "Detective Lieutenant McGee is upstairs. I'll connect you."

There was a moment's delay before McGee's voice rang over the wire.

"Who's been bumped?" he demanded without preliminary. The phone sergeant had informed him of the nature of the call. "Who's calling?"

"One moment," the man at the phone answered. "You'll do, McGee. I understand you're a good man. Have you the correct time?"

"What?" McGee snapped. "Are you kidding me?"

"Not at all, McGee. Have you the correct time, I asked?"

"It's two minutes after ten, if it matters. Playing jokes on the police department isn't a healthy kind of fun, let me tell—"

"Thank you. Mr. Leonard Leach has just been murdered in his home, McGee. The address is six-five-four-seven Maplewood Avenue, and it happened not more than thirty seconds ago. This is the murderer talking. My name is Thomas Townland, and I live at—"

"*What!*"

"I said, my name is Thomas Townland, and I live at five-nine-four Beechwood. Good night, Mr. McGee."

The killer coolly put down the telephone and turned to leave the room. He had heard quick footfalls come down the stairs, and now he saw Clarice standing in the hallway, staring into the sitting room. Her eyes were popping and the breath was gone from her. But as the murderer walked toward her she recovered her voice.

"Mr. Townland!" she screeched. "What have you done?"

"You can see for yourself," said the caller, "I've murdered Mr. Leach. Good night."

He brushed past the paralyzed maid, opened the front door, and walked out of it. In a moment the snarl of a starter sounded, and a car rolled away from the curb.

2

KILLED BY THE DEAD

A POLICE CAR screeched to a stop in front of the home of Leonard Leach. Two hundred pounds of sinew and brawn, named McGee, lurched out of it. He trotted to the door followed by Detective Sergeant James Baxter. Not fifteen minutes after the murderer's knuckles had tapped the door, McGee's hammy fist slammed at it.

McGee pushed in as the maid fluttered toward him. She was hysterical. All she could do was babble and point toward the sitting room door. McGee and Baxter stepped through it and came to a stop eying the dead man on the rug.

"It's straight, all right, Box-Car," McGee sighed. "I didn't believe it, but there's been a murder."

He took a close, quick look at the dead man. He turned back to find Clarice staring in, whimpering. McGee grabbed her arm and shot questions at her.

"Did you see it happen? Was it this Townland bird? Do you know why he did it? Where'd he go?"

Clarice gasped out the answers. "I was upstairs! It was Mr. Townland—yes. I let him in. I saw him coming out of the room with the gun in his hand after I heard the shots. I don't know why he did it. He got into a car and drove off!"

McGee barked to Baxter: "Grab that phone and signal the squad cars, Box-Car!" At the maid he snapped: "What kind of a car does Townland drive? You know the number? Never mind—the desk'll get that sooner than you can answer."

"It's a Luxcar," Clarice gasped. "Mr. Townland wouldn't drive anything else because he and Mr. Leach both work at the Luxcar plant."

"Doing what?"

"Designing motors and t-things. Oh, I—"

McGee kept on asking questions while Baxter put the call through to Headquarters, but he learned nothing more. When the maid began to sob so she couldn't talk, McGee gruffly ordered her upstairs to bed. He faced about grimly as Baxter left the phone.

"Damnedest thing I ever heard of—a man committing murder, then calling Headquarters and announcing it! I didn't believe it, but the maid says it was Townland, all right. You stay here, Box-Car—I'm beating it to Townland's place."

McGee thrust out the door and lumbered back to the police sedan. In a moment it was whirring over the pavement. Townland's address was registered on McGee's mind. He kept the horn blaring, took corners on two wheels, and sped past red lights. Townland's place was located in the same residential district, but McGee wasn't wasting any time.

Born skeptic that he was, McGee couldn't doubt that a man had been murdered in a most daring fashion. The big detective literally hailed from Missouri, which accounted for his sobriquet of "Show-Me," and he looked upon the

world with disbelieving eye: yet he couldn't bring himself
to doubt the startling announcement he had heard over
the phone, especially since it was backed up by the testimony of the maid of the murdered man. Still, there was
something about this amazing killing that made McGee
alert and wary.

In ten minutes he was braking the car to a stop in front
of the address of Thomas Townland. It was a small house,
and lights were burning inside it, in one room downstairs
and in one room on the second floor. McGee hitched
out his service gat as a precaution, loped to the door, and
hammered hard.

No answer came, so McGee grabbed the doorknob and
pushed. He stepped into the hallway, and looked around.
The house was quiet. The two rooms which opened to the
right and left were modestly furnished and empty. The
dining room and kitchen, McGee saw as he made the
rounds and listened, were also unoccupied. He turned to
the stairs.

A SLIGHT SOUND made him pause and listen. He was not
sure that he had heard anything, but he waited. It didn't
seem possible to McGee that a man would deliberately
inform the police that he had committed a murder, then
fight them off when they came, but nevertheless, distrust-
ing such theories, he took precautions.

He went up the stairs sideways, gun ready, glancing back
and forth. He heard no other sound, and he saw that the
upper hallway was empty. All the doors along it were open.
The first was a woman's room, obviously, but it apparently
had not been used in some time. The light McGee had seen
was shafting from the bedroom at the front of the house.

McGee stepped warily to the door, stopped short, and gasped. A man was lying on the bed, face up, his arms flung out, his coat thrown back. The shirt around his heart was stained red. An automatic lay on the floor at his dangling feet. McGee's first glance told him that this man was dead.

"Came home and killed himself," McGee muttered as he stepped into the room.

He bent over the bed. The dead man was about thirty-five, and not bad looking. McGee assumed that he was Thomas Townland, and verified this fact at once by the discovery of several letters which were protruding from the inner coat pocket of the corpse. They bore Townland's name.

McGee warily left the room and made a circuit of the upper floor. The guest chamber and the bathroom were also empty. In the woman's room McGee saw a photograph inscribed "With deepest love for my darling wife—Tom." The picture was that of the dead man, and that clinched the question of his identity.

Returning to the front bedroom, McGee studied the scene. He began to look troubled. His snap-judgment that this was a case of suicide, began to appear to be premature. There were no powder burns on the dead man's shirt McGee couldn't find a single charred speck. Had Townland held the gun even at arm's length and pulled the trigger, the broadcloth would certainly have been scorched. The fact that it wasn't made the theory of suicide untenable.

"Shouldn't 've thought so," McGee told himself. "Can't trust theories. This is murder."

His worry turned to astonishment. Bending over, he gave the bloodstain on the cadaver's shirt a close scrutiny, and made a disturbing discovery. The cloth was crusty with the dried blood. That meant that a considerable time had passed since the firing of the fatal shot. Not just a few minutes—longer.

McGee consulted his watch. It was now ten twenty-eight. Leach had been killed at a minute or so past ten. The murderer, if he had come directly to this house from Leach's place, must have arrived at ten or twelve minutes past. If Townland had been killed immediately, it could have happened only sixteen or seventeen minutes ago. And that wasn't long enough for blood to dry so completely as the stain on Townland's shirt.

McGee gingerly raised one of Townland's hands. A startled gasp came from him. The hand, the whole arm was rigid! Rigor mortis had stiffened the body. It meant that Townland's death had occurred earlier in the evening—much earlier.

"Good Lord!" McGee moaned aloud. "Townland was dead—certainly he was dead—long before Leach was killed!"

McGEE TRIED TO figure it out. Townland had died first, much before ten o'clock. But at ten o'clock Townland had killed Leach. How was it possible? Did Townland, dead with a bullet in his heart, drive over to Leach's place, shoot Leach, then return to his own home and die again? That, to judge from the condition of Townland's body and the Leach maid's testimony, was what had happened!

"Something," McGee told himself grimly, "is screwy!"

Show-Me McGee distrusted everything, including theories; he was skeptical of this whole business. Disdaining to jump at conclusions, he fell back on routine investigation. In an angry manner he bent over and glared at the dead man. In a moment his stern gaze reached Townland's shoes. They were muddy.

McGee made a note of that in his little black book, and looked further. The room, he saw, was not in good order, and the floor was dusty, as though Townland had been living alone in the place for a while. There were footprints in the film on the oak, some of which were patterned. Rubber-soled shoes had made them, McGee knew; perhaps a pair of golf-sneakers.

Townland's shoes were leather-soled. McGee opened the closet door and poked into it, searching for another pair which might have made the odd prints on the floor. He found none. Into his notebook went a line about the patterned prints.

McGee sighed, and trod downstairs, looking for a telephone. He found it in the dining room.

"Sullivan," he clipped out when he had connection with Headquarters. "Here's another murder." McGee gave the dead man's name and address. "Where're Nelson and Stone?" These two gentlemen were, respectively, the Medical Examiner and the fingerprint expert.

"Both over at Leach's place, Show-Me," said Sullivan.

"Buzz 'em to come over here as soon as they can," McGee asked. "If Redman and Samuels aren't busy, send 'em out, too." They were plainclothes men with whom McGee and Baxter had been playing pinochle earlier in the evening. "And if this thing pans out the way it looks, you'll be reserving a padded cell for me in the nut house."

McGee lowered the phone and paused. His eyes became alert as he listened. Very faintly came a sound. From the hallway, McGee judged. He heard a faint tap, as of a sole hitting a stairstep—and then nothing.

McGee slipped his service revolver back into his hand and pretended to go on talking over the telephone.

"No, Sully, I haven't any idea who did it. The house is empty except for Townland. There's not much we can do until the fingerprint expert gets here."

And while he *ad libbed,* McGee listened. The faint tapping sound came again—another step taken. Someone *was* coming down the stairway quietly, trying to sneak out of the house while McGee telephoned. McGee leveled his gun, kept talking, and waited.

An almost inaudible rattle came from the front door. Swiftly McGee bounded into the sitting room. As he sprang toward the hallway door he saw a dark figure opening the front entrance. It was a man, half out. As McGee's heels thumped, he gasped and darted away.

McGee went after him like a stampeding elephant. His man was halfway across the porch when he flung himself out the front door. One bound brought him close enough to throw his beefy arms around the fugitive. There was a brief, sharp struggle. McGee thrust his captive against the wall and poked his gun into the young man's stomach; and that ended it.

"Oh, you don't have to go home so early," McGee panted. "Stay and have some beer and pretzels."

The young man was white as death. McGee had knocked the breath out of him. He blurted:

"I didn't have anything to do with it!"

"That's what they all say," McGee answered. "What's your name?"

The answer came readily enough: "Washburn—David Washburn."

"Uh-huh. And you were hiding in the house all the time I was in there."

"Well—yes, I was. I didn't want to get mixed up in it, that's all. I was hiding in a closet, but—I don't know anything about it."

"Go back in," McGee ordered.

Washburn breathlessly went into the house. McGee followed him into the sitting room, gun still leveled. He turned on a light and took a closer look at Washburn. About thirty, he judged, and clean-looking—no earmarks of the criminal about him. McGee commanded him to sit down, and he sat down.

"Tell your story," he ordered. "But don't expect me to believe any of it."

Washburn was cooling off and growing composed. His story seemed straightforward enough to McGee. He explained that he had come to the house to see Townland, had received no answer to his knock, but, since the lights were on and the door unlocked, he had risked going in. Drawn upstairs by the light, he'd found Townland dead on the bed. He'd arrived only a few minutes ago, a little after ten, and—

"When?" McGee demanded.

"About ten fifteen, I guess. I was rattled, and I didn't know what to do. I decided to leave, and I was just going out, when I saw your police car stop in front of the house. That rattled me still more, and I hid in the closet. I know it was crazy, but I didn't want to get taken to Headquarters

and questioned—because I have something very important to do."

"WHAT'S MORE IMPORTANT than reporting a murder?"
McGee demanded skeptically.

"I came here trying to find Townland—because Sylvester Morrison is missing. He's the father of the girl I'm
going to marry. He didn't come home for supper tonight,
and I've been trying everywhere to locate him. Patsy—she's
my fiancée—is worried sick. Townland was a friend of her
father—we all work in the same place—the Luxcar plant."

"What?" McGee snapped. "Morrison, too?"

"He's the Chief Automotive Engineer there. I'm an
assistant. Townland was another engineer, so—"

"And a man named Leach was another?" McGee interrupted.

"Yes. We all worked in the shop. We've been developing
a new motor. Townland was a good friend of mine—I've
been here before and I didn't think coming in would—"

"Wait a minute!" McGee snapped, his eyes shining.
"How many other engineers are there working together
in the plant?"

"That's all—in our shop," Washburn answered. "Listen.
I tell you I don't know anything about what happened
upstairs. I told Patsy I'd phone her from here—I came
straight from her home. Can I make the call?"

McGee said: "Lift your feet." When Washburn
complied, puzzled, McGee studied the young man's shoe
soles. They were smooth leather. They couldn't have made
the odd prints in the bedroom.

"You don't look like a murderer to me, but I don't trust

appearances," McGee remarked. "I might take a chance on you—but I'll make that call myself."

McGee made the call. Very quickly a girl's voice answered. He identified himself to Patricia Morrison.

"Mr. Washburn hasn't been able to locate your father, and he's come to me about it. First—what time did Mr. Washburn leave your place tonight?"

"Just ten," the girl answered. "He's been searching for father ever since eight o'clock. Father should have been home by seven fifteen, but he didn't come, and I haven't heard from him—I'm terribly worried!"

"Did he ever show up missing before?" McGee asked.

"No—never. Father's hours have been a little irregular lately, but he always phones me before he leaves the plant. Tonight he phoned at seven and said he was coming right home. But he didn't come—and by eight o'clock I was so worried I phoned David—Mr. Washburn—and asked him—"

"Now," said McGee gravely, "don't you worry. I'll be over soon and find out all about it. You be hunting up a good picture of your Dad, and write out a full description of him, including what he was wearing today. Just in case we've got to broadcast—"

"Do you think father was kidnaped?" asked the girl.

"Me, I don't think unless I have to. It makes for trouble," McGee answered. "You just sit tight."

As he hung up he heard the whine of tires outside. A car was drawing to a stop near the curb. As two men climbed out of it, a second car braked behind it. Two others appeared out of the second sedan, and the quartet, talking, came toward the door of the house.

"You stick by me, Washburn," McGee said to the young man. "Just for luck I'll frisk you, but I don't expect to find anything."

He didn't. Assured that Washburn was concealing no weapons as well as no untruths, McGee opened the door. The four men who came in were Dr. Nelson the Medical Examiner, Stone the fingerprint expert, and Redman and Samuels, both detectives.

"Busy night, doc," McGee said. "You come upstairs with me and take a look at the stiff we've got here. I've got to know something about him."

McGee gestured Washburn up the flight and followed the doctor. In the bedroom the six men gathered, while the Medical Examiner went to work on Townland. Dr. Nelson pursed his lips critically.

"How long, doc," McGee asked, "would you say he was dead?"

"He must've got it about eight o'clock," the examiner answered.

"Sure?" McGee insisted. "He couldn't 've stopped that bullet along about fifteen or twenty minutes after ten?"

"Not possibly," Dr. Nelson declared. "No, not possibly."

"THAT MAKES IT nice," McGee said with a grimace. "Then I've got the job of figuring out how this dead man went to another house and killed a guy, and then came back. Because this is the bird that killed Leach at ten o'clock, doc. That's what makes everything so lovely."

"Leach—Leach is dead!" The exclamation came from David Washburn. "Oh, God—if something's happened to Patsy's Dad—"

"Yeah, I know," McGee interrupted him. "Two Luxcar

engineers get killed on the same night, and you think maybe the third has got it, too. Now, don't go jumping at conclusions. So far, all we know is that Morrison is missing. I'm looking into that right away."

McGee, with a gesture, turned the place over to Redman and Samuels. With Washburn he trod down the steps and out the front door. Washburn's car was parked out of sight beside the house, in the driveway, and McGee elected to take the police sedan.

He started off silently, his mind mulling over the problem of how a dead man could have committed murder. Washburn was too worried to talk. They reached the Morrison home without having spoken, and McGee led the way to the door. In answer to his knock Patricia Morrison appeared.

"I'm McGee," McGee said, just as a telephone somewhere in the house jangled loudly.

The girl spun about and hurried along the hallway. McGee went after her quickly and grasped her arm. As the phone chattered again he said:

"Steady, now. I'll take it."

While the girl watched him anxiously, and Washburn put his arm across her shoulders, McGee lifted the receiver and said: "Hello!"

Over the wire came a single short sentence:

"Look in the mail box."

Then the line went dead.

McGee jerked and clattered the hook. He kept clattering it angrily until the operator answered.

"Trace the call that just came in here," he snapped. "Police work—snap it up!"

He thrust the instrument at Washburn and strode out the door as the girl's eyes followed him wretchedly. On the post of the gate McGee saw the mail box. He thrust one huge hand into it, felt an envelope, and jerked it out.

The sheet of paper it contained was covered with pasted newspaper clippings. Each word was separate, some in small type, some taken from headlines. McGee hurried into the house with it as Washburn turned from the telephone.

"The operator says it came from a pay station. The number's—"

"I expected that!" McGee snapped. "Now, listen—Morrison's been kidnaped, right enough. You leave this to me!"

He read the patchwork of words rapidly:

> Your father is safe and will not be harmed if you follow directions. Get ready $100,000 as first payment and evidence of good faith. Make it small old bills and don't dare mark the money or it will get you nowhere. Directions for delivering it will come to you by telephone, and if you make it impossible for us to negotiate your father will die. You must pay $500,000 if you want him back alive.

There was no signature.

"Half a million ransom!" McGee gasped. "Great Lord, what makes 'em think he's worth that much?"

Within a few hours he was to learn the answer to that question.

3

WORTH A BILLION

SHOW-ME McGEE LUMBERED into Headquarters at eight the next morning. He had been sitting up all night with the case, and he was disgusted with the world in general. Wearily he trudged along the corridor from the street, entered a room, and strode toward the desk.

Sergeant Sullivan was writing in the book while a patrol-man and two battered-looking men stood before the grille. Sullivan was saying: "Disturbing the peace" when McGee signalled him. He left the book and came through the gate.

"Any word on where Sprice is?" McGee asked him.

"Not yet," Sullivan answered. "Michaels and Roark are pussyfooting after 'em and we ought to have news soon."

"Let me know the minute we hear," McGee stipulated.

He stood a moment in thought as Sullivan returned to the desk. As he turned and left the room, the Desk Sergeant asked one of the two unkempt men a question:

"What's your name?"

"Henry Wilson," said the man. "My name is Henry Wilson."

McGee climbed the stairs and went into his office. Detective Sergeant James Baxter was there, half asleep in a chair. He yawned and indicated McGee's desk. On the blotter lay Baxter's report. McGee pushed it aside and took up the telephone.

He called the Morrison home, and the missing man's daughter answered.

"Any word yet from the kidnapers?" he asked.

"No—not yet," Patricia Morrison answered, her voice unsteady.

"You let me know as soon as you hear," McGee reminded her sympathetically. "Be a good girl now."

As he put the phone aside the door opened and a patrolman looked in.

"Mr. Kilgore's waiting to see you, Show-Me. Shall I bring him in?"

"Not yet. I'll let you know."

As the patrolman withdrew, McGee took up Baxter's report and put it down again.

"I can't read all that stuff now, Box-Car," he sighed. "You tell me about it."

Baxter made a noise. "Show-Me, it's a lulu," he said. "Whether Townland was dead at the time or not, he killed Leach. What's more, Leach killed Townland before Townland killed *him*. All the evidence points to it."

"Talk sense!" McGee snapped.

"I'm telling you," Baxter insisted. "First, take the evidence that Townland killed Leach. The maid saw him—eyewitness. Townland phoned you himself and told you he'd done it. Then take Townland's shoes. There's a wet spot in the ground by the curb in front of Leach's house, and Townland's footprints are in it. That checks against the mud on Townland's shoes.

"To clinch it, the bullets in Leach came from Townland's

gun. Townland had a license for that gun. It was the one you found in the bedroom with him. The serial number checks with the license. Townland's fingerprints are on it. It's Townland's gun, all right, and the bullets that killed Leach came out of it.

"You couldn't want more conclusive evidence than that, Show-Me."

"No," said McGee with a moan.

"Now, take the killing of Townland," Baxter went on. "The prints of the rubber-soled shoes in Townland's room were made by Leach's shoes. I found the golf shoes that made 'em in Leach's closet, and the maid says it was his favorite pair. Leach was in Townland's bedroom and made those prints.

"I FOUND A gun that belonged to Leach in Leach's place. It was hidden deep in a dresser drawer, and it'd been used recently. Leach also had a license for it, and the serial number of the gun I found checks with the license. No doubt of its being Leach's gun. Well, also, the bullets taken from Townland's body were fired through that gun."

"So?" McGee said.

"So," Baxter said, "there's no way of getting away from it. Leach went to Townland's place and killed Townland in the bedroom. Then went back home. After that, Townland went over to Leach's place and killed Leach."

"When he was dead," McGee said.

"When he was dead," Baxter nodded. "I asked questions of Townland's neighbors. It seemed they heard something that might have been a shot along about eight o'clock. As usual, everybody thought it was a car backfiring. But the

time checks with Doc Nelson's idea of when Townland got
it—eight o'clock."

"Where was Leach at eight clock?" McGee asked.

"The maid says he was out, she doesn't know where."

McGee rubbed his face. "It doesn't make sense," he said.
"From all I can find out, those men were good friends. Had
been for years. There hadn't been any falling out about
anything. No reason for either of 'em killing the other."

"Seems so," Baxter agreed. "I was trying to smell out
some love tangle, but there isn't any. Townland's wife is
visiting her folks in Minneapolis. Leach's wife was playing
bridge at a regular weekly session of a hen card club. Both
of 'em are straight. No jealousy or anything like that there."

"There wouldn't be," McGee opined. "This is linked
up with the Morrison snatch. Two automotive engineers
killed and a third kidnaped on the same night—and all
of 'em working for the same plant. That means plenty."

"What's your slant on it, Show-Me?"

McGee sighed. "My old man, rest his soul," he answered,
"was one hell of a good cop. He taught me to believe about
half of what I see, a quarter of what I read, and a tenth
of what I hear. That goes in this case. I don't believe it. It
didn't happen."

"Those guys are certainly dead, Show-Me," Baxter coun-
tered. "All the evidence shows that Leach killed Townland
first, then Townland killed Leach; I know it doesn't make
sense, but you can't get away from it."

"It didn't happen," McGee said morosely. "Anything
in this report, Box-Car, about fingerprints on the Leach
telephone?"

"Two sets of prints on it," Baxter answered. "The maid's and Leach's."

"Any of Townland's?"

"No."

"Why not? He used that phone when he called me. Was he wearing gloves or something? If he was, what was the idea—why should he want to keep his fingerprints off the phone while he called up and reported he'd just killed a man?"

"I don't know, Show-Me."

"Neither do I, Box-Car. Now, you step out and ask Mr. Kilgore to come in here and talk to me about this. And you hang around, Box-Car. I'm intending to go pay a call on Silk Sprice pretty quick, and when I go I want you with me."

"Sprice?" Baxter asked. "You think he's behind this, Show-Me?"

"I don't think anything about this case," McGee retorted.

MR. SPENCER KILGORE was an impressive man. His hair was prematurely silver, his bearing poised; and he radiated an air of success and power. Well he might, for he was president of the great Luxcar Corporation, and there were millions of Luxcars on the road. He was one of the most distinguished business men of the country.

This morning he was agitated. He entered the office with quick step, gripped McGee's hand hotly and, when he sat down, he perched on the edge of his chair.

"Mr. McGee, I want you to understand that I will give you every possible assistance," he declared. "It is too late to do anything for poor Townland and poor Leach, but in the case of Morrison—I will gladly pay the ransom person-ally, out of my own pocket, if it will insure his safe return."

"Half a million, Mr. Kilgore?" McGee asked.

"Half a million, and more if necessary," Mr. Kilgore affirmed emphatically.

"That's good," McGee remarked. "The Morrisons haven't got any money. They couldn't pay any ransom. Looks to me like this snatch was aimed at you, Mr. Kilgore—aimed to make you pay."

Kilgore flushed angrily. "I haven't any doubt of it," he asserted. "The amount of ransom demanded makes that obvious."

"But it isn't obvious to me yet why a man like Morrison is worth that much money to you," McGee answered.

"If Townland and Leach were still alive, he wouldn't be, to put it frankly," Kilgore answered. "But with both of them dead, Morrison's safety is worth—I should say, Mr. McGee, that Morrison's life is worth a billion dollars to the Luxcar Corporation at this moment."

McGee sat up. "A *billion?* A quiet little man like Morri-son is worth a billion to you? Why?"

"Because he is the only man now alive who—because he alone can—" Kilgore broke off under stress. "Mr. McGee, can I speak to you in absolute confidence?"

"You can."

But even then Kilgore hesitated. It was evident that his mind was weighted heavily. He pursed his lips and strug-gled with his thoughts; but abruptly and swiftly he began to speak.

For years, he explained, the Luxcar Corporation had maintained a special research shop quite apart from the engineering staff which devoted itself to the development of new sales-stimulating gadgets for their new models. It was located in a remote part of the plant, it was equipped with scientific precision tools unequaled elsewhere, and it was kept constantly under armed guard.

The utmost secrecy surrounded the activities within the four walls of the special research shop.

The work there was in charge of Sylvester Morrison, who was Chief Automotive Engineer for Luxcar, thoroughly trustworthy and one of Luxcar's oldest employees. Leach and Townland had been his assistants, and they were just as reliable. The nature of their newest work was not even known to their own families.

David Washburn, Kilgore explained in answer to a question from McGee, was an assistant engineer, but he did not work in the special research shop. Only Morrison, Leach and Townland were ever admitted, other than Kilgore himself and a few other officers of the corporation for whom he could vouch.

"Sounds like something pretty important has been going on in there," McGee remarked.

"Important? The most important development in the history of motorcar manufacturing, Mr. McGee!"

For several years, under Morrison's direction, the special research shop had been perfecting what Mr. Kilgore termed a "super-powerizer," The exact nature of this he was not free to divulge, but he hinted that it was a radical departure in carburetation combined with a radically redesigned motor. Its purpose was to extract from ordinary motor fuel a far higher percentage of energy than heretofore had been thought possible.

Mr. Kilgore explained swiftly that the present-day auto-mobile was a most inefficient contraption. The gasoline motor in its present stage of development was able to extract only a very small part of the power latent in the fuel used. The rest was sheer waste—power paid for by the purchaser of gasoline, but squandered in countless ways.

The chief loss of power was due to improper vaporiza-tion of the fuel, and it was upon a remedy for this defect that the special research engineers had been laboring.

"The super-powerizer and the new motor are almost perfected. I say 'almost' because the final application of the new principles has not yet been fully solved. But success is assured, and within a few months we expected to put the first of the new superpowered models on our proving grounds. Recently Morrison assured me that the new car will easily get one hundred miles to the gallon of gasoline."

McGee sat up again. "A hundred miles to a gallon of gas! Baby!"

"EXACTLY," MR. KILGORE agreed grimly. "The phenom-enal mileage is only one advantage of the super-powerizer. It removes a dozen other disadvantages of the present-day motor. You can easily realize the tremendous potentialities of the device, Mr. McGee. Think, for instance, of having to refill your ten-gallon gas-tank only once a month on the average."

"I'd certainly buy me one of those cars!" McGee declared.

"So would millions of other motorists, McGee. The commercial value of the super-powerizer is beyond calcu-lation to the Luxcar Corporation. It will render obso-lete every automobile on the roads today, as well as every airplane, every gasoline motor in existence. It will revolutionize the industry—and Luxcar will reap all the benefits.

"No doubt you know, Mr. McGee, that there is an agreement among some motor-car manufacturers concerning new developments. Improvements designed by one manufacturer, according to the stipulations of the blanket contract, soon become the property of the others. You have seen this work out with free-wheeling, ride-control, and other gadgets. Luxcar, Mr. McGee, has never been a party to this agreement."

"Then that means no other motorcar manufacturer will be able to use your super-powerizer! You'll have 'em all licked!"

"Exactly," Mr. Kilgore said again. "We will rule the motor-car world. If we kept full control of the super-powerizer, and only Luxcars were equipped with it, the Luxcar would soon be the only automobile sold in the world.

"If we licensed other manufacturers to use it, we would be paid enormous royalties. Either way, Luxcar will rule supreme in the industry and the device will bring billions of dollars to us."

McGee was wide-eyed. "What can you do now—with Townland and Leach dead, and Morrison being held by kidnapers—"

"Nothing," Kilgore said with a snap. "Exactly nothing. There are no blueprints, and what records there are have been kept in a code which only the three engineers knew. Even if the code were deciphered, the most important part of the work would still remain to be done. The model itself would be an enigma to new engineers. They would find themselves in virgin engineering territory—bewildered and helpless.

"Any one of the three research engineers would have perfected the super-powerizer working alone. But with Leach and Townland both dead, Morrison is the only man alive who can complete the job. That, Mr. McGee, is why Morrison's return is worth so much money to us."

"So that's it!" McGee exclaimed. "That's it!"

"You understand," Kilgore went on, "I don't suspect any rival manufacturer of this. It would get them nowhere. The patents already taken out, on component parts of the super-powerizer, protect us from that. No one but Luxcar can benefit from the super-powerizer as matters stand. But not even Luxcar will benefit if Morrison is not safely returned."

"This isn't the work of business rivals, Mr. Kilgore," McGee agreed. "This is the work of slick crooks—slick as they come.

"They saw a billion-dollar chance, and they took it. Somehow news of that super-powerizer leaked out, Mr. Kilgore."

"No doubt. The devilish part of it is, McGee, that the crooks didn't even need to know the details of the device. All they needed was a hint of its value and that it was nearing completion. That much might easily have leaked out. McGee. What in God's name can we do?"

"That," said McGee, "will take a bit of figuring. If you're willing to back me up—pay the ransom if necessary—"

"Yes, of course! Anything! At all costs we must get Morrison back safely."

McGee sighed. "Sweet job, looking for him. No picture

of him to go by. His description has 'average man' written all over it. He might be almost anybody you see on the street.

"One thing's sure—he's tucked away in some nice, safe place. All we can do is wait, Mr. Kilgore—wait for the kidnapers to send word—follow a few hunches—and pray."

The telephone rang as Kilgore rose. He mumbled his thanks, received McGee's assurances, and left the office. McGee picked up the telephone and heard the desk sergeant's voice.

"Sullivan, McGee. Michaels and Roark just reported. Sprice and every danged one of the Devil's Dozen are in Sprice's place. What's the move?"

McGee's eyes glittered. "I want about four cars full of tough cops, Sully," he said. "We're all going to pay Mr. Sprice a social call. Get your men mobilized. I'm coming down."

"You think this is Sprice's trick, Show-Me?" Sullivan asked.

"I don't think much at times like this," McGee answered. "I don't trust thinking. Only, I know that whoever planned this job is as slick as Satan. Mr. Silk Sprice answers the description... And, Sully. If any word comes from Morrison's daughter, I want to know about it the quickest way."

McGee, scowling, heaved his two hundred pounds out of his chair and trudged heavily out the door.

4

BLIND ALLEY

FOUR POLICE SEDANS paraded out of the Headquarters garage. They wheeled into a through street that led into the center of the city and went quietly on their way. Behind the wheel of the first sat Show-Me McGee.

"Why're you figuring Silk Sprice is behind this, Show-Me?" asked Sergeant James Baxter, who was slumped at McGee's elbow.

"Sprice," answered McGee, "has been feeling the pinch. He's about through in this man's town. He's planning on lighting out, and it would be just like him to pull a trick like this before taking it on the lam."

"Yeah," Baxter said, "but, still, how're you figuring it? It's proved that Leach killed Townland, and it's proved that Townland killed Leach, so—"

"When you claim a dead man committed murder two hours after he got a bullet in the heart, that's some proof!" McGee snapped. "Box-Car, you believe too much."

"Well, if it didn't happen, what did?" Baxter demanded.

McGee answered the question with grim silence. The string of police cars was proceeding down a broad avenue lined with apartment houses. McGee swung to the curb in front of one which sat on a corner. The second car stopped

behind him; the third and fourth wheeled into the side-
street and stopped there.

Twenty men got out of the cars. Some of them, by
McGee's prearranged plan, moved to the service entrance
of the building and others sauntered into the alleyway
and stopped near the base of the fire escape. McGee left
others in the lobby, and took half a dozen with him into
the elevator.

One of them was Michaels. Roark, Michaels told
McGee, was in the basement, inside the service entrance.
At the eighth floor landing, two men lingered while
McGee and the others trod past an angle of the corridor
to a green door. On the green door McGee knocked.

"Want to buy a set of books?" he asked when the door
opened. "I'm woikin' me way t'rough colletch."

Silk Sprice was looking out. "Hello, McGee," he said.
"Hello, boys. Well, isn't this jolly. Come right in."

He was dapper, tall, poised. Entering, McGee found the
room full of men. The air was blue with smoke and half
a score of ash-trays were filled with half-burned butts.
The dope was straight: the Devil's Dozen were holding a
conclave. McGee glanced them over: as slick a crowd of
unscrupulous criminals as he'd ever seen assembled under
one roof.

"You boys figuring out how to boost the Sunday school
attendance?" he asked.

They laughed. Silk Sprice laughed the loudest. McGee's
men closed the green door and spread out along the wall,
also laughing. McGee teetered on his toes and looked
them all over.

"The boys and I," Sprice explained, "have just been

talking over a little trip. We're all good friends and we think we'd like to travel a little. What do you think of it, McGee?"

"Swell," McGee said. "The farther you go the better I'll like it. Leaving soon? I'll give you a basket of fruit to take along. Maybe a few pineapples."

They laughed again. This time McGee did not. He turned about, faced Sprice, and waited until the room was quiet.

"Well, Silk, where is he?"

"Where's who, McGee?"

"Morrison."

Silk Sprice smiled. "Quit your kidding," he said.

"Am I kidding?" McGee asked. "I didn't think I was. I want to know, where is Morrison?"

"You mean the old bird the papers say was snatched last night?"

"I mean the old bird the papers say was snatched last night. And that's one thing in the papers that can be believed."

"McGee," said Sprice, "I don't know."

McGee glanced about. The Devil's Dozen were smoking silently, ringed around him, watching coldly. McGee felt like a mouse inside a circle of twelve hungry cats.

"I'm paying you a compliment, Silk," McGee said to the chieftain of the crooks. "This is a big job. It's the biggest snatch that's ever been pulled. I'm here because I think you did it."

"Thank you, McGee, but your praise is misplaced."

"Half a million ransom asked, Silk. That would put a new lining on you boys' pockets, wouldn't it? A real grand finale before you lam out of town."

"Sorry, McGee."

McGee's eyes glinted. "In that case, Silk, I'll treat you to an automobile ride through our fair city. Down to Headquarters. The whole crowd's invited."

Sprice scowled. "Don't be a damned fool," he snapped. "We're not in this snatch, and you know it."

"That's just what I don't know. I tell you, I'm paying you a compliment. It took brains and nerve to pull this job, and you've got 'em both. Let's talk it over at Headquarters."

Sprice crushed out his cigarette. "Wait a minute, McGee! I've read about this thing in the papers. It happened early last night, didn't it?"

"If a dozen different clocks weren't wrong, it did."

Sprice was facing McGee squarely. "What time was Morrison snatched?"

"A little after seven."

"I was at the banquet at the Claremore last night at seven. So were all the boys."

McGee looked surprised. "Were you? *All* the boys?"

"Ask your men," Sprice suggested. "Ask Michaels, here. He was there. He saw us."

McGee looked at Michaels. Michaels nodded.

"WE WENT INTO the banquet a little before seven, and it was after eleven when we left," Sprice explained. "In case you happen to think we pulled the two killings, too, McGee, that lets us out of everything."

"Things happened at seven, eight and ten o'clock," McGee said. He looked again at Michaels and asked: "Is that straight, Mike? The whole gang was there from before seven until after eleven?"

Michaels nodded again. "All twelve of 'em, Show-Me.
Every one of 'em stuck it through."

McGee blinked. He was familiar with the way the
Devil's Dozen worked. They were a closed corporation.
No outsiders were running in on any of their jobs. It was a
certainty that no outsiders would have been brought into
a plan so important as this billion dollar snatch. With all
the Devil's Dozen accounted for during the entire evening,
McGee found himself stalemated.

"Well?" he said sheepishly.

"You're too good a man to be pulling a boner like this,
McGee," Sprice remarked.

"I think so myself," McGee retorted with a shade of
anger. "Well, so long, boys. Drop me a picture post card
while you're gone."

He opened the green door and went out. His men filed
after him, and the door closed again. Heavy footfalls moved
away down the corridor.

The twelve men in the room were silent while they heard
the elevator buzz up and down again. One of them sidled
into the hallway and came back, gesturing that the cops
were gone. Silk Sprice lighted a fresh cigarette, thoughtfully.

"Half a million ransom," he mused.

"Lucky for us we were at that banquet last night, Silk,"
remarked Ace Slaton wryly. "Getting hooked for a job we
didn't pull wouldn't be so funny."

"Half a million ransom," Sprice murmured again.

"This snatcher is either crazy," opined Beefy Burgess,
"or else this Morrison is worth plenty of potatoes to somebody."

"If he's worth half a million," Sprice said softly, "why isn't he worth a million?"

Eleven pairs of hard eyes studied him. Sprice's mind was working, planning. They could see the alert calculation in his eyes, the tenseness about his merciless mouth. He turned to peer at Ace Slaton, and he peered at Ace Slaton a long minute.

"Before those flatfeet barged in here, Ace," he said, "you were talking about that snatch. You were saying—"

"Nobody that belongs in this town pulled that job, Silk," Slaton answered quickly. "It's big time. It's slick. There's only one bird I know of who'd plan a snatch like that."

"Who?"

"Wings Williams."

"Where," asked Silk Sprice softly, "is Wings Williams?"

"He had an apartment with his pal, Twisty Newton, over on Fairfield," Slaton answered. "Only, he hasn't been there for the past week. I've heard that he's left town. But it don't look like he's left town. Not with a snatch like this being pulled."

"Williams and Newton work alone, don't they?"

"Yeah—and with half a million to split between 'em. Not so bad."

Silk Sprice sat down. "Ace, wander over to Williams' old place on Fairfield. Try to find out where he lammed. Beefy, ease over to the Calumet Club and try to find out what they know about Williams over there. The rest of you boys pick up what you can. Don't let any flatfeet trail you around, either. Beat it, now."

They were peering at him.

"Lay it on the line, Silk," Ace Slaton urged.

Sprice seemed not to hear. "I'll meet you boys at Blackie's tonight, early—say eight. I'll have it worked out by then."

"I got you; Silk!" Ace Slaton exclaimed in a hushed tone. "We snatch Morrison from Williams. We collect the ransom. The cops won't be looking for us in the job because we've already cleared ourselves. Geez! There's a layout!"

"Beat it!"

Avid eagerness shone in the eyes of the eleven. They exchanged quick glances. Of one accord they moved toward the door, with that silent, unified stealth which marks the predatory animal going on the prowl. They sidled out, and closed the green door behind them.

Alone in the room, Silk Sprice sat still. His cigarette burned unnoticed in a tray. His eyes gleamed as his shrewd mind planned.

"Half a million ransom," he said in a whisper. "And if he's worth that much he's worth a million cool."

A PARADE OF four police sedans swung into the Headquarters garage. Men piled out of them. Show-Me McGee wriggled from the wheel of the first, making disgusting noises.

"I thought you knew about that, Show-Me," Michaels said to him. "Didn't anybody tell you?"

"I remember somebody telling me," McGee answered drearily, "but I don't believe much of what I hear."

"You can lay it down as the straight dope. This is no job of Silk Sprice's."

"I believe it now," McGee moaned.

Baxter fell into step with him as McGee ambled toward the door which connected with the main building.

"Anyway, Show-Me," Baxter said, "four dozen Silk Sprices don't figure in when the evidence proves that Leach killed Townland and then Townland killed Leach and—"

"Quit saying that, will you?" McGee snapped. "You want to drive me nuts?"

As he strode past a door, Desk Sergeant Sullivan's voice howled: "Show-Me! There's a girl on the phone, all excited and asking for you."

McGee spun, crashed through the gate of the desk, and snatched up Sullivan's phone. The sergeant at the switchboard plugged him in. It was Patricia Morrison.

"Had word?" McGee asked quickly.

"Yes—just a few minutes ago. A man called. He said to get the money ready. He said to keep the police out of it." The girl's voice was anxious. "He threatened to kill my father if—"

"They all do that," McGee told her gruffly. "Don't you worry about it. The police are already in it—all the way in. What else did he say?"

"But if father is in danger—"

"Young lady," McGee reminded her sternly, "alive, he's worth a potential half million to the kidnapers. Dead, he's not worth a nickel. Don't forget that. What else did he say?"

"But if Mr. Kilgore is willing to pay the ransom—and he was here this morning and said he is, more than willing—"

McGee sighed. "I don't want your father killed," he said. "I want him brought back. But also, it's my job to get the kidnapers. This is not just a plain snatch case. There're two murders involved, and I can't overlook that. Now, come on—what else did he say?"

The girl hesitated. "He said to get the money ready. He

said if it's not in old, small bills it won't do any good. He said if the money's marked he'll destroy it. He said to do it up in a bundle and wait until tonight for further orders."

"Tonight?" McGee asked.

"Yes. But he said if any police come to the house, word won't come. He said if we don't act in good faith, father'll never be sent back. Even if I leave the house, he said—"

"He's making it tough," McGee remarked. "He's playing a desperate game, and we'll have to do what he says. All right, you telephone Mr. Kilgore and tell him to bring the money. You stay right there at the house, and no cop's 'll come. But when he phones again, I want you to call me the minute he hangs up."

"I will," the girl promised.

"Don't you be scared, now," McGee reassured her.

McGee put down the phone and paused in thought. As he leaned on the desk, a blue-uniformed man strolled in from the corridor. He asked Sullivan: "What's the dope on that pair who came in this morning for disturbing the peace, Sully? One of 'em gone?"

"Yeah, the big one, Max Smith. Both of 'em got fined ten bucks, and Smith paid up. The other one couldn't, so he'll be our guest for the next ten days. Henry Wilson's his name."

Baxter was looking across the counter at McGee.

"I don't like this, Box-Car," McGee said. "That girl's got a right to be worried. The penalty for snatching in this state is life, and a smart lawyer can get a man off with life for a killing. There's not much choice. If it gets too hot for the snatchers, they'll put a bullet into Morrison and try to beat it."

"I want to know how the snatchers figure in," Baxter said, "when it's proved that Leach killed Townland and then Townland killed Leach—"

"Oh, God!" moaned McGee. "Quit saying that! I'm worrying about Morrison. I'm worrying about that girl. If I pull a boner, and that poor kid loses her Dad, and Kilgore loses a billion bucks, I'll never be able to look myself in the face again. It'll kill me."

"What're you going to do, Show-Me?" Baxter asked as McGee came through the gate.

"What the hell can I do?" McGee snapped. "No evidence to work on. No way of figuring it out And you, standing around, babbling things about Townland killing Leach and Leach killing Townland! You're a good guy, Box-Car, and I like you. But if you say that again I'll slam you a lulu on the nose!"

5

NIGHT TRAIL

THE BIG CLOCK on the wall, its face shining white in the electric light, was ticking toward the hour of ten. Beneath it sat Show-Me McGee, scowling at a sheet of paper on which words clipped from newspapers were pasted. Attached to it was a brief typewritten report:

> No finger-prints. Clippings all from local papers of the past four days. Common library paste, used, impossible to trace. Envelope cheap, very common variety. No leads here.

"Yeah. No leads anywhere," McGee muttered to himself. McGee had been mulling over the case the entire day; all day he had cooped himself in his office and waited. It was the waiting which wore on McGee's nerves. And these unhopeful reports were no help.

> Morrison was seen to leave Luxcar plant a few minutes past seven, p.m. Walked into parking-space apparently to get his car. Man at gate did not see him leave. No later reports of his movements.

That was another, and there was a third:

Kidnaper called from chain drug store downtown corner Third and Main. Phone used by hundreds. Impossible to trace.

The telephone jangled and McGee grabbed at it. The Phone Sarge said over the wire, "It's the girl again, Show-Me!" The voice of Patricia Morrison followed.

"Mr. McGee—he called again, a minute ago!"

"Good! What'd he say?"

The girl talked swiftly; "He said to take the money to the Memorial Bridge and throw it over the rail within ten minutes."

"Mem—! Ten minutes?"

"Yes. He said if it isn't thrown over within ten minutes at the outside, he won't touch it, and it will be fast. He said, for me to take it there, alone, and to drop it into the water."

"Is this guy a fish or something?" McGee demanded; "It'll sink. If—"

"He told me to make it waterproof and fix it so it wouldn't sink. I can use the oil-cloth off the kitchen table, and there's an empty motor-oil can in the garage I can wrap up with it. But it'll take me five minutes to get to the bridge and—"

"Good girl—that's fast thinking," McGee applauded. "He said ten minutes so we won't have time to make any plans for collaring him. And he won't touch it, either, if he's suspicious. You go ahead and do as he said."

"He said if the police interfere, or if I don't throw the money from the bridge in ten minutes, I may not hear from him again. He said if I make it dangerous he'll—"

"Young lady, it's my moral duty to keep this kidnaping

from turning into another killing. You do as you're told, and get there on time."

The line clicked, and McGee pushed the telephone away, his eyes narrowed. He grabbed up his hat and loped out the door, thinking at top speed; This snatcher, he reflected as he lumbered down the stairs, was certainly a smooth customer. This throwing-the-money-in-the-river business was a new and unexpected trick. How the devil could the kidnaper get it out of the river, anyway?

McGee hesitated in the lower corridor.

The snatcher couldn't be figuring on using a boat—boats are slow, and it would be too dangerous. He certainly wouldn't try swimming—he could be spotted easily. Then what? McGee didn't know.

He did know that one word to the police radio announcer would send every squad car in the city skirting along both banks of the river as it curved past the city. The kidnaper must know that, too: he was too clever not to have taken it into consideration. The squad cars were no good. Besides, they might mean the death of Morrison.

McGee trudged into the police garage as he thought it over. He'd have to take it alone, and play safe. That decided, a new thought struck him. He whirled, raced back upstairs, jerked open a drawer of his desk, and snatched up a pair of binoculars. Clutching them, he sped back into the garage and wedged himself behind the wheel of an official sedan.

He whirled into the street, blared his horn, and shot in the direction of the river: The near bank was a long, narrow park, with a broad boulevard running parallel with the water. It was a preferred residential and business section in which tall buildings reared, overlooking the park and river. McGee skidded into the boulevard and raced in the direction of the Memorial Bridge.

The distance was short. The ten minutes had not yet expired. McGee swung into a side street, slammed his car to a stop just past the corner, dodged out, and sprinted into the entrance of an office building.

AN ELEVATOR, CONTAINING a sleepy operator, was open at the lobby level. McGee sprang into it, and barked commands, flashing his badge. The cage shot up. At the tenth floor level, McGee hurried out of it and ran toward the end of the corridor. At the end of it a window over-looked the river.

The operator was following McGee. McGee snapped at him: "Turn out those lights!" As a switch clicked and the corridor filled with darkness, McGee stationed himself at the window. He put the binoculars to his eyes and peered down at the Memorial Bridge.

It was a white span across a band of black. Traffic over it was light at this hour of the night. A car hummed across it, toward the center of the city, and was gone. For a moment the bridge was empty. McGee glanced at his watch and saw that the ten minutes were almost up.

Alert, he saw a light coupé swing from the boulevard and turn onto the bridge. It proceeded slowly. As it reached the center it stopped altogether. McGee saw a girl step out of it quickly—Patricia Morrison. She was holding a bundle in her hands.

Quickly she tossed it over the rail of the bridge. It arced down and struck the water with a splash. McGee did not turn his binoculars again toward the girl, though he knew she was getting back into the car and driving off. He kept the overlapping circles of his vision on the blob which was floating on the black surface of the river.

For a moment the bundle drifted slowly in the shine of the bridge lights. It began to move more quickly as the current caught it and bore it along, away from McGee. It passed outside the area of light and became harder to follow. McGee kept his eyes on it, puzzled and grim. He was still unable to figure how the kidnaper intended to get hold of that hundred grand.

McGee did not see that now Patricia Morrison's car was off the bridge and running along the road at the other side of the river. He did not see that another car was creeping over the span, following it. It turned in the same direction, but let the girl's car gain on it.

It turned about quickly, and recrossed the bridge. Swinging into the boulevard, it rolled slowly near the curb, in the direction the river was flowing. Half a mile farther on it stopped, and its lights blinked out. There it waited.

Ten stories up, McGee kept his binoculars trained on the bundle floating with the current. It was moving more rapidly now, in the center of the black band of water. Where the river turned past a bend, the bundle began to bob closer to the opposite shore. McGee knew that it would not come to rest anywhere along the bank; the current was too fast for that. But it was floating closer and closer toward the bank.

It was hard to follow in the darkness. McGee stood rigid and scarcely breathed. He could see a faint, irregular splotch on the surface, and that was all. Suddenly he caught his breath. The package was moving more quickly now. And it was swinging closer to the shore. Presently, to McGee's surprise, it began to float upriver, against the current!

It was being drawn, somehow, to the opposite shore of the river. Abruptly it disappeared altogether in the darkness of the overshadowing trees. McGee waited only to spot the location; then he whirled about and sped back to the elevator.

His snapped commands, prodded the operator into making a quick trip to the lobby level. McGee trotted out of the building, to his car. Making a quick U turn, he darted into the boulevard, shot along a block, and swung toward the curb to make the turn across the Memorial Bridge.

He spurted over it, turned again, and proceeded more cautiously along the opposite shore-road in the same direction. He saw no car ahead of him. His headlamps showed him the only pedestrian was an old woman pattering along the left-hand side of the road and carrying a market basket. McGee slid on and, when he reached a spot near which the floating bundle had disappeared, he stopped the car and got out.

Snuggling his service revolver in his hand, he trotted across the band of grass which stretched between the road and the water. On the bank he paused, looking up and down. There was no sound except the hum of the city, no movement anywhere. McGee began to prowl.

He was thirty yards downstream when he saw something white on the ground and sprang toward it. Snatching it up, he saw that it was a section of oil-cloth large enough to cover a kitchen table, and wet. Near it lay an empty gallon oil-can and lengths of twine which had been cut.

The kidnaper had been here; he had stripped the covering from the bundle and slipped away.

McGee moved closer to the water. His feet became entangled in something and he cursed, trying to kick it free. Reaching down, he felt strong cord caught in his shoe-laces, and he dragged at it. Something moved in the grass in response to McGee's pull. A moment later he had it in his hand—a long pole. A cheap but otherwise orthodox bamboo fly-casting rod.

That was it. The kidnaper had waited here, where the current would bring the floating bundle close to the shore. Casting the line out with the fly-rod, he had been able to catch the hook in the oil-cloth covering the package. Drawing it in then had been a simple matter.

McGee made angry sounds, dropped the rod, and trotted away from the water's edge. Certainly the kidnaper had been on this spot within a few minutes. If he had left a car parked near, he could be well away by now. But a parked car might have attracted attention; it would have been a risk, and this kidnaper wasn't taking any unnecessary chances. Perhaps he had walked away. But if he had—

THE RIVER-BANK WAS darkly shadowed by the over-hanging trees, but there was small opportunity to hide. McGee trotted to the edge of the road and peered up and down. There was no car in sight, no pedestrian in sight, except the old woman. Except the old woman! McGee's gaze fastened on the doddering old figure grimly.

She was walking toward the Memorial Bridge, a slow-moving figure clad in bulky skirts. She was plodding straight on, without looking up from the road. McGee had to admit that she fitted into the surroundings. Farther down the river there were cheap stores, and all along the opposite side of the road were the drab houses of a cheap district. The old lady was evidently going home from a market.

McGee's inborn skepticism took hold of him. He went to his car, and turned it around. He drove toward the old lady slowly, and let the headlamps of the car play upon her. She moved aside, but kept on plodding. McGee drew alongside her and called out the door.

"Want a lift, mother?"

The old lady looked up and said sweetly: "No, thank you. I'm almost Home now."

McGee took a breath and gave the motor gas. Behind him, in the rearview mirror, he could see the old lady still shuffling along. She turned, presently, crossed the road, and walked toward a group of houses. As she disappeared in the shadows, McGee passed the Memorial Bridge.

Just beyond it he stopped the car, cut the ignition, and turned off the lights, He adjusted his mirror and kept his eyes on it. Long minutes passed. But, finally, the old lady reappeared on the sidewalk, head still bent, market basket still on her arm, shuffling along.

Headlights gleamed upon McGee as a car turned from a side street onto the river road. It slowed down, drew to the curb, and paused. The old lady also paused. She shot a quick glance up and down the street. The near door of the car swung open, and she climbed in. The next moment the car was rolling on its way.

"Ah!" said McGee. "I knew I couldn't trust appearances!"

He started up again swiftly, turned around, and began to follow the car into which the old lady had climbed. It was moving rapidly. McGee used only his parking lights, and gave it plenty of headway. Another bridge spanned the river in the lower section of town, and this the other car crossed.

McGee buzzed after it. It proceeded around the business district of the city, and turned into a through street. Warily, McGee turned one block behind it, and spurted to the next corner. Slowing, he saw the other car pass a block away. He spurted, slowed again, saw the other car once more pass the intersection on the next street. In this fitful way McGee kept it in sight.

When it reached the juncture of another through street, it turned. McGee also turned. He kept well back of it until it swung left. Again he gave it a block's distance, and kept up this procedure until the car reached a sparsely settled district. When the chase took another angle, McGee was forced to follow on the same road.

Abruptly the car swung off the tar onto a new dirt street. McGee went past. A hundred yards farther on, blanketed from sight by a treed bend, he U-turned and came back. When he passed the dirt street again the car was gone.

McGee drew to the curb and got out. He walked along the street. There were only two houses in the first block, after which there was open country. One of the houses was dark; in the other a light came on as McGee watched. He fondled his service gat again, and eased toward it.

Following the driveway, he crept to the side of the house. The shades were drawn; he could not see in. Faintly, he heard voices inside, but he could distinguish no syllable. McGee meditated crashing the place, but paused. Circling quietly to the rear of the house, he found a slanting cellar door. He pried at it, and it lifted.

At the base of the stone steps McGee found another door, and this one was locked. The first skeleton key McGee tried drew the bolt. He found himself in a dark cellar, facing a flight of wooden stairs which rose to another door. McGee eased his two hundred pounds carefully up those stairs, and listened.

The voices were clearer.

"No, nobody, I tell you," a man was saying. "Somebody offered me a lift, but that was nothing."

Another male voice answered: "Say, you could pass yourself off as Greta Garbo if you tried it."

"Here—take this stuff."

"Where we going to keep it, Wings? It's a lot of coin to stash away somewheres."

"Is it? Well, there's plenty more coming, Twisty. We'll get the whole half million, don't worry about that."

McGee's tense hand raised to the doorknob. Silently he twisted it and pushed. The door was firm. McGee stooped, squinted through the crack, and saw that the door was held by a bolt.

Footfalls were coming into the hallway into which the cellar door opened.

McGee gripped his gat. He drew himself back, gathering all the power of his husky frame to hurl it against the panels.

6

MAN OF MANY FACES

McGEE'S TWO HUNDRED pounds of muscle battered against the door. His first thrust tore from the jamb the screws which held the bolt-socket. The door whipped open and McGee went through with a rush.

He was in the rear of a dimly lighted hallway. Light was shafting across it from a room at the front of the house. A man was standing in full sight. His hand flashed to his hip pocket as McGee stampeded in.

McGee's gat flashed twice, and the thunder of the reports made the house shake. His two-legged target fired at the same time and leaped aside. Plaster dust spurted out of the walls behind McGee as he crouched in the corner to spring. His man was on the stairs now, clambering up.

McGee darted forward, peering through the banister at the swiftly swinging legs above. He crashed a bullet at them, saw one rocket toward him, and heard wood splinter. He leaped on, fired again, and flung himself toward the base of the stairs.

The man on the steps had whirled around. He blazed away twice as McGee came into full sight. McGee grunted as a slug nicked his ear, dropped to his knees, and pulled his trigger once.

The man on the stairs screamed. He turned, started to run up, missed his step, crashed against the rail, and came spilling down. His gun dropped from his hand and lay on a top step. McGee whirled against the wall as a movement sounded behind him.

In a doorway a grotesque figure was standing, jerking an automatic toward him. It was the figure of the old woman from the shoulders down—bulky skirt, baggy sleeves and all—but above the neck was a head with a man's haircut. The automatic spat at McGee as he ducked.

He had two bullets left, and he contributed one to the masqueraded man in the doorway. A shrill yell mixed with the thunder of the report. The skirted figure fell back. McGee stepped across the hall swiftly, and as he reached the sill, fire splashed into his face.

The flame of the automatic stung his skin, and the bullet creased across his cheek. McGee's gun was level at his waist when he pulled the trigger. A breathy gasp came from the grotesquely costumed man as he tottered back. He struck a chair, spilled backward over it, and lay in a crumple of up-thrown skirts that disclosed ancient shoes and fancy silk socks.

McGee whirled back. The man at the bottom of the stairs was moaning, but not moving. The other was never going to move again. McGee fished bullets out of his vest pocket, reloaded his gat, and took a deep breath. Stepping to the man in the hallway, he made sure that no other gun was concealed. Climbing the steps, he picked up the dropped automatic.

Grimly he proceeded to search the house.

McGEE FOUND ONLY one thing that interested him. It

was a huge make-up box which sat on a dresser in one of the bedrooms. It was filled with supplies of skin-dye, grease-paint sticks, false hair, spiritgum, fish-skin, creams, and everything else an expert make-up artist could desire. Everything in it had been used. McGee looked it over with sour amusement.

He found no kidnaped man. The attic, all the closets, and the cellar yielded no clues that Sylvester Morrison had even been in the house. When he finished his search, McGee returned to the front downstairs room where the skirted man lay dead.

On the table sat the market basket and, beneath a layer of newspaper, lay neatly packeted bundles of banknotes. They would amount to a hundred thousand and they would go back to Spencer Kilgore. But it was of Sylvester Morrison that McGee was thinking.

He trod back to the hall, picked the squirming victim of his bullet off the floor, carried him into the room and deposited him on a davenport. McGee studied his face.

"Twisty Newton," he said. "I thought you'd left town."

Newton moaned. McGee bent over the masqueraded man on the floor. Cunning applied greasepaint and deftly penciled lines covered the features of Wings Williams, but McGee recognized him. He turned back to find Newton sitting up, cuddling a punctured arm.

"Hurt?" McGee asked.

Newton whined.

"Where're you keeping Morrison?"

Newton whined again.

McGee sat in a chair facing him. "Two murders and a

snatch, Twisty. That means you can get the electric chair twice and then get sent up for life. How'll you like that?"

Newton exploded. "I never croaked them guys! I never had anything to do with it!"

"Then that leaves life," McGee said calmly. "If anybody believes you. And I don't. I don't trust lots of things, Twisty, including you."

"Williams done it! I tell you I never—"

"Uh-huh. Williams can't argue with you about that now. It's the chair for you, Twisty. Except maybe if you tell me all about it—and where you're keeping Morrison."

"Williams croaked them guys," Newton gasped. "It was his big idee. I told him we couldn't get away with it. I told him—"

"How'd he work it, Twisty?" McGee demanded.

Newton glared at him. "What'll it get me if I tell?"

"Keeping quiet will get you the chair, Twisty, if that's any answer. Maybe you can convince me you didn't croak them two guys. I'm a hard man to convince, but maybe you can do it. If you do, you'll get off easier."

Newton whimpered and held his arm. McGee's hard gray eyes were piercing him. They were forcing him to talk.

"Wings Williams planned it all out," Newton mumbled. "He found out about the whole business. He—"

"Killed both Townland and Leach."

"I tell you I wasn't in on that! Wings went to Leach's place first, see? He sneaked in and got Leach's gun and golf-shoes, see? Then he went over and bumped Townland.

"He took Townland's shoes and Townland's gun. He went back to Leach's place, sneaked in again, and left

Leach's gun where he found it and Leach's shoes. That was easy—there wasn't nobody at home but the maid."

"Then?" McGee asked grimly.

"Wings came back here and made up like Townland. He was a wizard at it. Was on the stage. He went to Leach's place and killed Leach, then he beat it to Townland's house, put the shoes back on Townland, and left the gun."

McGee nodded. "The lights in Leach's place were dim. The makeup wouldn't be noticed very quick. Twisty, I guess I believe you—so far."

"What reason I got to lie now? I'm tellin' you what happened. I ain't goin' to fry for what Wings done."

"Wings didn't pick up Morrison alone, did he?"

Newton's face blanched. "Naw," he said. "I helped him with that, but that's all I helped him with, see? Wings planned it all out. He put our car in the Luxcar plant parking space, see? We waited for Morrison to come out. Wings'd fixed Morrison's car so it wouldn't work, and he was goin' to offer a lift."

"And it worked out."

"Naw. Naw, it didn't. Somethin' funny happened. Morrison come out a few minutes after seven. He come walkin' slow, and actin' funny, like he didn't know where he was goin'. He looked around like he couldn't find his car, and there it was right in front of him.

"Wings grabbed him quick and put him in our car. He kept actin' funny. Didn't make no resistance. He sat there and looked funny and didn't say a word. Then after we got him here Wings figured somethin' 'd gone wrong in his head, and he called Doc—a doctor."

McGee's eyes were narrowed.

"What did Doc Reitz say?" he asked.

"He said it was amnesia or somethin'. He said it was loss of memory from overwork. Morrison couldn't even remember his own name. It must've come on him sudden. He didn't know nothin' about hisself. So Wings thought that was a lucky break, and he made a new plan, see? Oh, God, I got to have a sawbones for this arm!"

"I'll take care of that, Twisty—when I hear the rest of it," McGee said, grimly curbing his impatience.

"So the next morning Wings made me go downtown with Morrison early, see? It was a chance, but there wasn't many people around. I waited till a cop come along, then I hit Morrison, and he begun to fight me, see? The cop grabbed us and took us in. I give my name as Max Smith, and Morrison gave his as Henry Wilson, because Wings'd made him think his name was Henry Wilson, see?"

McGee jerked up. *"What?"*

"So I paid my fine, see, but Morrison couldn't pay his because we'd took his money away, so he's staying in the jug, see? Wings figgured nobody'd ever think of lookin' for him there. Wings figgured he was an ordinary-lookin' little gink and nobody'd spot him. There was a chance, but it was safer 'n keepin' him hid somewheres. So all this time he's been down at Headquarters, see? Locked up. Ow! I got to—"

"For the love of God!" McGee moaned. "You're telling me that Morrison is in a cell at Headquarters, not knowing who he is and thinking his name's Henry Wilson."

"That's what I said, ain't it? That's all I done. I never croaked them two guys. I got to have a doc—"

McGee reached out, fastened fingers in Twisty Newton's shoulder, and jerked him to his feet.

"You and me," he rasped, "are going down to Headquarters right now!"

He thrust Newton into the hallway. Newton whined as he stumbled, pushed toward the outer door. McGee followed him grimly.

Suddenly a blast shook the house. Thunder seemed to rock the walls on their foundations, and filled the rooms deafeningly. Twisty Newton screamed in terror. His legs bent under him swiftly, and he thumped to the floor with blood spurting from his neck. McGee staggered back and fell while the echoes rattled.

The door was shaking. Round holes were appearing in it and splinters were flying. A fusillade of bullets was drilling through.

IN THE DARK outside the door four guns barked in unison. Flame flashed against the woodwork as a grim quartet emptied their weapons through the panels. Then they spread apart and stood back, listening.

No sound came within the house.

"Both of 'em dropped!" one of the men said huskily.

Another reached out to try the door. Silk Sprice's voice rasped at him.

"Keep your mitt off that knob! Let it go! We scram!"

The four men spun about. They loped off the porch and darted to a car standing at the curb. Silk Sprice sprang to the wheel as his three henchmen clambered in behind. The sedan spurted off.

Houses were few in this section. If the shots had attracted attention, there was no sign of it yet. Sprice took advantage of the quiet when he swung the sedan into the new road; he drove slowly, back toward town. In the rear seat the three men peered about, their guns reloaded and ready.

"Listen," Sprice said over his shoulder. "Ace, you beat it over to the hideaway. Grab that case and put it in the car. Spike, go with him and handle the Tommy gun."

"Geez! What's up!" Ace Slaton exclaimed.

"Listen, I told you!" Sprice snapped. "Beefy, get the rest of the boys. Snap it up. I'll meet you at the corner of Broad and Sycamore—got that? Wait outside the drug store. Be there as fast as you can make it."

"Sure, Silk, but—"

"Jake, stick with me, but when I stop, grab a phone. Tell Greasy we want two cabin planes waiting on the field right away. Tell him he's going with us, and he's going to keep his mouth shut. The planes are for you mugs. I'm sticking here in the hideaway with Morrison."

"With Morrison!" Ace Slaton gasped. "You heard what we heard! Morrison's in a cell at Headquarters."

"I heard what you heard, all right," Silk Sprice answered grimly. "You boys could see a little coin, couldn't you? We're ready to lam it out of here anyway. Well, we're getting the coin and we're getting plenty. Bring those masks, too, Ace."

"Geez, what a chance!" Slaton breathed.

"Chance? Not much of one," Sprice answered smoothly. "You don't know the half of my plan yet. You just know we're going to cash in on a million dollar baby, that's all."

The car was humming straight for the heart of the city.

7

PITCHED BATTLE

RED LIGHTS FLASHED on the switchboard behind the desk in Police Headquarters. Sergeant Bill Lewis plugged in and began to speak. A high-pitched voice interrupted him.

"Headquarters! This is Kilgore, at the Luxcar plant. There's a riot out here. There's a strike. They're swarming in the plant, breaking up machinery. For God's sake, send your men out!"

Lewis jerked up. His routine duty was taking reports from call-boxes, listening to complaints about noisy neighbors, and hearing about lost children. This was different.

"I got you, Mr. Kilgore! How many're makin' trouble out there?"

"Thousands of men! They're wrecking the plant! Hurry your men out here!"

The connection broke. Lewis gasped over his shoulder to Sullivan, "Riot call, out at the Luxcar plant!" and at the same time another red light flashed.

"Help!" came a feminine squeak over the line. "They're setting fire to the buildings! They're breaking down the fences and smashing the windows! Help!"

"Who're you?" Lewis gasped.

"I'm the night switchboard operator—Luxcar plant. Oh, hurry. Somebody'll be killed!"

Lewis half rose and barked at Sullivan: "Who's here to give orders?"

"Nobody—give 'em yourself!" Sullivan roared.

Lewis picked up plugs and jabbed them into sockets in the switchboard rapidly. Sullivan sped out of the room and across the hall, into the broadcasting station. Shouts rang through the corridors.

"Riot call!"

The police machinery snapped into high.

Detectives and patrolmen scrambled into the garage. Starters snarled. Motors whirred. Cars began shooting out of the garage doors, sirens screaming. Black Maria lurched into the mad cavalcade. Traffic stopped. Pedestrians scattered. Traffic cops' whistles shrilled. Riot call!

At a hundred points about the city the loudspeakers in the city's squad cars began to blare.

"Calling all cars! Calling all cars! Riot at the Luxcar plant. All cars proceed to Luxcar plant! Calling all cars!"

A hundred motors burst into action and a hundred prowl cars began screaming toward that outlying district in which the great Luxcar plant was situated.

Riot call!

One of the squad cars shot past the intersection at Broad and Sycamore Streets, a few blocks from Headquarters. In front of a drug store four men stood watching it. One of them was Silk Sprice; the others were Ace Slaton, Beefy Burgess and Spike Leary.

It was Sprice who had just called the fake alarm over the telephone and given the name of Kilgore. It was Ace

Slaton's falsetto that had sounded like a terrified woman to Sergeant Lewis.

It was Beefy Burgess who had just wriggled out of a booth after flashing a third fake alarm.

"Bolice?" he had gulped. "I am de man who runs de grocery store near de Luxcar plandt. You bedder send help. Dere's bad drouble!"

As the squad car shrieked away, the four men moved alertly toward the sedans waiting at the curb. Inside them eight other men were waiting. Sprice took the wheel of one of the cars: Ace Slaton took the other. They spurted away in the direction of Headquarters.

When they came to a quick stop in the street in front of the big brick building, ten of the men were wearing heavy black masks. Ten of them were gripping automatics, ready for action. Sprice masked his face before he leaped out. Ace Slaton, also masked now, sprang to his side.

"Split!" Sprice commanded. "Take it quick!"

A group of masked men darted along the corner to the side entrance of Headquarters. Another group spurted toward the open doors of the garage. A third trotted to the main entrance of the building.

Just inside the garage, the one pack of masked men stopped. They slapped the doors shut. They sprang toward the corners of the cavernous room, levelling their weapons.

"Stick 'em up!" they rasped. "Keep 'em up! Lively!"

Four startled mechanics obeyed orders as one of the masked men shut the door which connected with the main building. Black guns waved threateningly at them, demanding silence.

Desk Sergeant Sullivan was trying to get a call through

on the phone when two masked men popped in through the door. One of them shoved his gun through the grille into Sullivan's face.

"Drop it! Back up!" he commanded.

The other slipped through the gate;, menacing Sergeant Lewis with a glinting gat. He shoved it hard into Lewis' chest and thrust the sergeant back against the wall. With his free hand he reached out and tore three plugs from their sockets, breaking the connections.

"Stay there!" he ordered.

TWO OTHER MASKED men hurried to the door labeled *Broadcasting Station.* They thrust in, startling the announcer who was standing by the microphone, and the technician who was keeping an eye on his dials near the window. One of them slashed his gun through the air and crashed it against the announcer's head. The other leaped to the technitan, clapped a hand over his mouth, and pressed a gun over his heart.

The first of the masked pair inspected the dials swiftly, then stepped to the microphone.

"Calling all cars," he droned harshly. "Calling all cars. Regardless of developments, remain at the Luxcar plant until further orders. Instructions straight from the Chief. Calling all cars...."

He stepped back, clicked a switch that disconnected the microphone, and aimed carefully. The room rocked with the roar of his exploding gun. A huge amplifier tube in the corner of the room crashed to bits, and water spurted out of its shattered jacket.

"Sit tight!" he ordered the two captives, waving his gun.

Two more men bounded up the stairs to the second

story. They whipped open the Chief's door and found the office empty. Two other offices they discovered to be deserted. When they thrust into the third, two detectives leaped to their feet.

The two masked men pushed them into a corner, grabbed away their guns, and backed to the door.

"Take a rest," they advised.

Another pair, downstairs, strode toward a door at the rear end of the corridor. They opened it, looked inside, found two blue-uniformed men inside. Racks of rifles hung on the walls. Ammunition was stored on shelves. It was the Headquarters arsenal.

"Steady!" one warned the two cops.

The other snatched a black object out of his pocket and hurled it. He followed it swiftly with another. The biting fumes of tear-gas gushed into the air, filled the room. The two men stepped back, slammed the door, turned the key in the lock, and stood on guard.

Silk Sprice and Ace Slaton advanced along the corridor of the lower floor shoulder to shoulder, guns leveled. The rest of the Devil's Dozen were swiftly and silently following through Sprice's swiftly arranged plan. So far the attack had been made without alarm, with only one shot fired; but now the men in the gas-filled arsenal room were shouting and choking.

Sprice and Slaton strode past the barred cell doors which lined the rear of the corridor. Opposite the arsenal was another ordinary door, closed. It jerked open as the muffled shouts of the trapped men sounded in the corridors. Two blue-outfitted men hurried out.

"Up!" Sprice commanded.

One of the cops was a gray-haired patrolman. He snatched at his service revolver. Sprice's gun barked sharply, once. The old patrolman threw back his head, fell to his knees, dropped flat to the floor.

Ace Slaton's gun was on the other. "Take that as a lesson, dummy!" he rasped. "Get the keys! Snap it up!"

"I haven't got 'em!"

"Get those keys!"

A bullet blasted past the patrolman's ear. Sprice sprang toward him, snatched the gun out of his holster, and gave him a stinging slap across the face. The maddened man struck back wildly, throwing himself on Sprice. Sprice's gun spoke.

The second patrolman dropped, holding his stomach. Sprice spun about. There was a man at the connecting door of the garage. There were two more in the desk room. There were two more outside the arsenal. The others were not in sight, but every means of exit, every means of communication was blocked. Sprice snapped at Slaton:

"Find those keys!"

Through the barred doors of the cells faces were peering. Slaton glanced at them quickly, and his gaze stopped on a small, grayed man who looked out dazedly. Slaton gestured toward him; Sprice nodded. Slaton sprang toward the desk room.

Sullivan and Lewis were still at bay before the guns of the two other masked men in the room.

"Do you hand over the keys," Slaton rasped at the Desk Sergeant, "or do we walk over your dead body?"

Sullivan did not move. Lewis sighed at him: "Give 'em the keys, Sully. We can't stop 'em." Then Sullivan moved.

He lifted the ring of keys from his desk and tossed them through the opening in the grille.

Slaton snatched them up. He raced down the corridor to the cell in which the timid little man stood. He selected a key which was numbered to correspond with the number on the cell door, inserted it in the lock, and turned it. The bolt drew back.

Muffled reports shook the door of the arsenal. One of the cops inside was firing through. The two black-masked men guarding the door stepped apart, and their automatics blazed flame. The shooting behind the door stopped.

Slaton slammed the heavy cell door open. He grabbed the small man's wrist and dragged him out of the cell.

"Come on, baby!" Sprice ordered. "We won't hurt you. You're worth a million to us!"

Sprice and Slaton, with Morrison between them, hurried along the corridor toward the main door. Near it Sprice paused. He put his fingers to his lips and blew a shrill whistle. It was the signal to his men that the job was done. It was the signal to scram.

A POLICE SEDAN came streaking down the street at a crazy speed. Its horn was blaring. Pleasure cars darted aside to give it way. Pedestrians scrambled for the curb. As the sedan streaked past they saw in the front seat a man whose face was half blood, who was staring ahead grimly, whose hands were whitely clamped to the wheel.

Show-Me McGee swung his car around the corner while the tires whined. Because he was driving with one hand, with his left arm hanging limp at his side, he gave the wheel too little twist. The sedan thumped against a curb and climbed upon it before McGee braked it to a stop. He scrambled out and headed for the front entrance of Headquarters.

He was dizzy, and his body was throbbing with pain. Besides his punctured arm he had a gash in his side. That much punishment he had been unable to avoid before leaping out of the hallway and away from the door through which death had been drilling. He had dragged himself to his car and, Morrison still on his mind, had come speeding back to Headquarters.

But now he found the big front entrance closed. As he loped toward it he heard the blasting of shots inside. He paused and dazedly looked around. Near the curb in front of the building he saw two heavy, expensive cars. Silk Sprice's wagons! McGee realized their engines were running; and shots rang again inside Headquarters.

McGee paused. He slopped his revolver into his hand and trod cautiously toward the door. Just as he reached to take its knob he heard a shrill whistle inside. An instant later the door began to open.

Two masked men appeared in the light. McGee blinked at them. They stopped, dismayed; and their guns flushed up. McGee was faster. His revolver spat twice. One of the masked men wheeled back, yelling. The other slapped the door shut.

Within the building a shout lifted.

"It's McGee! Get McGee!"

McGee scrambled to the curb. He could see, from there, that all doors of Headquarters were closed. He began walking backward, eyes grimly narrowed, gaze shifting from the entrance to the front of the garage. As he backed, the garage door inched open and the snout of an automatic appeared.

McGee slammed a bullet at the crack. Another bullet spat at him, but the crack closed. McGee spun about, and sprang for the nearest of Sprice's automobiles. He dropped behind the wheel, glanced swiftly to see that all but one of the windows were closed. The exception was at his left elbow. He cranked it to within an inch of the top swiftly.

The front entrance of Headquarters jerked open again. A masked figure appeared, aimed at McGee, and fired twice in swift succession. Two white stars appeared in the non-shatterable glass near McGee's head. McGee, raising his gun to the slit, answered the attack.

Swiftly he grabbed the wheel, stepped on the gas, and sped the car toward the front entrance. The wheels jounced over the curb. McGee slammed the car to a stop as it nosed at the door. The wood of the panels split as the bumper wedged against it. Five thousand pounds of automobile jarred to rest and barred the door.

McGee watched the garage entrance as he rapidly slipped new cartridges from his vest pocket into the revolver. The big door opened and two men sidled out. They fired at McGee and whirled away. McGee let them fire. This boat of Sprice's was a mobile fort. They couldn't touch him.

McGee swung the cylinder in place, eased down the opposite window, and threw two bullets as the masked men darted for the other car. One of them got it in the leg and sprawled on his face. The other lurched forward and spilled half across the running-board. A third masked man, coming out of the garage door, fired at McGee and retreated.

Bullets slammed down on the top of McGee's car. He reached out, shot upward wildly, and ducked out. A window above him was open. He fired at it again. Through it he caught a flash of two men locked arm in arm, struggling, one masked and one a detective McGee knew. McGee let it go at that, watched the garage door, and sprang toward the other car.

Inside Headquarters—bedlam!

SPRICE WAS SHOUTING hoarsely in the corridor. Ace Slaton was lying dead inside the main entrance. The two men he had stationed at the arsenal door had darted into the garage. Morrison was halfway up the stairs, huddled low. Shots rang on the second floor as two of Sprice's masked lieutenants hurried from the desk room.

Sergeant Sullivan and Sergeant Lewis went into action together. Sullivan grabbed a gun out of his top drawer. Lewis jerked his from his holster. They sprang toward the corridor in time to see the pair disappearing into the garage. Sprice was in the connecting doorway, yelling.

"The side way! The side way!"

Sullivan fired wildly at Sprice as Sprice whipped around. Bullets clashed across the corridor. Sullivan lurched backwards as a bullet took him in the shoulder, but he kept his balance and fired again, back to the wall. Lewis, at his side, blazed at the door opposite. Sprice vanished behind it.

Lewis darted to the rear of the corridor, where the side door was located. He turned the key in the lock, and thrust the key into his pocket. He was legging it back when he heard the high-pitched snarl of a motor outside.

McGee had reached the other car. With the windows closed all around him, he wrenched the sedan toward the curb. It lurched onto the sidewalk, and McGee shot it close alongside the building. Squarely into the broad door of the garage he eased it so that, from bumper to bumper, it blocked the way out. As he slid to a stop, the garage door opened and a masked man fired point-blank at McGee.

The glass turned white with a thousand cracks, but it held; and McGee laughed. He scrambled out the other side of the car, and darted past the corner of the building. Nothing was happening at the side entrance. He jerked to a stop at the window which looked into the desk room, and saw powder-smoke rolling in the corridor beyond.

McGee crashed his gun against the window, tapped out the saw-tooth edges, and heaved himself through. He lumbered into the corridor, saw Sullivan braced against the wall, Lewis crouching beside the door. Upstairs there was the blast of a shot, and a triumphant yell. The next instant Detective Mallory came bounding down.

"Both of those devils are out. Billy's got it in the leg. Where're the rest of those devils?" he shouted.

"They're all in the garage!"

McGee rasped: "Who else? Any of the boys?"

"The mechs."

"If you can get 'em out alive, get 'em. Otherwise they're going to do a lot of crying," McGee snapped.

He loped down the corridor, paused, and looked at the two still blue-uniformed figures on the floor. Sadly he wagged his head, put his own gun in his pocket, and picked up the weapons of the two dead patrolmen. Then he whipped around to the arsenal door.

Stinging gas gushed into his face when he opened it. Two men were lying on the floor, gasping, their faces streaming with tears. McGee choked, grabbed the arms of one of them and dragged him out. Then the other. McGee crammed his nose in the bend of his arm, ducked in, and came out sliding a box of tear-bombs.

The men in the corridor rushed for them.

"They'll get out into the street!" Sullivan gasped.

"Can't," McGee told him. "Alley windows too high. Get those mechs out if you can."

Nobody moved. McGee levelled both guns at the door and pulled the triggers as he advanced. The panels became perforated with black holes. He reached out one leg and kicked. He kicked again. The door flapped open, and McGee fired through it.

"Come on out, boys!" McGee yelled. "We'll keep 'em off!"

Black-masked men were crowded near the car door of the garage. They blazed at the opening that McGee had provided. Bullets sang through, into the corridor, and spanged against the brick walls. McGee lurched back as Sullivan, Lewis and Mallory heaved tear-gas bombs far over.

Terrified yells answered the bursting of the bombs. From the maze of cars at the rear of the cavernous space, brown-coveralled mechanics darted. Shots blazed again as they sprang through the door into the corridor. One fell with a pierced leg. Two more leaped through safely. A fourth hung in the shelter of a near car.

McGee spun two bombs through the door, at the cluster of black-masked men.

The mechanic dashed in.

"Heave 'em!" McGee blurted.

BOMBS RAINED INTO the garage. Bullets pancaked against the walls, flicked through the door. Some of the gas was billowing through. McGee ducked low, reached out with his left hand, fired swiftly with his right, and slammed the door shut.

"They'll get out!" Sullivan sputtered again.

"Sully, I tell you they can't," McGee roared. "We've got 'em. What the hell's been happening around here, anyway?"

A bullet splintered through the connecting door, and then no more. Inside the garage was a chorus of coughing, moaning, whining. McGee stepped close, flat against the wall.

"Listen, you mugs! You can come out this way if you come with your masks off, your hands up, and your guns in your teeth with the clips out!"

There was a scramble across the cement floor. The men in the corridor divided themselves on the sides of the door. The knob rattled, and a man darted out. His hands were up, and his mask was off. He was Beefy Burgess, and hot tears were scalding his face. In his teeth, butt outward to show the missing clip, he had his automatic.

"Open those cells! Herd 'em in!" McGee ordered.

Sullivan hastened to follow orders. He found the ring of keys on the floor and hastily unlocked every empty cell. The others kept their positions. Two more men trotted out, gasping, in complete surrender. And then McGee saw Silk Sprice stumbling through.

Sprice's arms were raised, his mask torn down, and he

had a clipless gun in his teeth. McGee faced him grimly, and took the gun away.

"You're a special friend of mine, Silk," McGee said, "so I'll lock you up in a special cell all my own self."

Sprice, blinded with tears, choking, turned away. McGee limped after him down the corridor. Sprice's arms went down slowly. McGee did not see that the movement put a gun into Sprice's hand. It slipped out of his sleeve, nestled snugly in his palm—a small automatic.

Sprice whirled like lightning and fired. McGee saw the spin start, saw the gun coming up. He fired the instant Sprice's gun let go, and his bullets splintered Sprice's gun-arm. Sprice's bullet ripped through McGee's baggy trousers and spattered against the floor.

McGee reached out, grabbed his tie.

"I shouldn't 've trusted you!"

He thrust Sprice into a cell, banged the door shut, and waited until Sullivan turned the bolt. Sprice sprawled out on the cot, half unconscious with pain. McGee peered at him grimly.

"I'll be gettin' you a doctor right quick, Silk," he said. "You've got to be well and healthy again for a trip to the chair."

McGee limped off, and found that all the others had come through. They were being herded into cells. McGee looked around dazedly, sighed, and shuffled into the desk room. He lowered himself into a chair and his eyelids drooped.

"Who's this guy?" Lewis shouted to anyone. "He came out of a cell, didn't he? He's in for ten days, isn't he?"

McGee blinked up at the timid little man whom Lewis had collared.

"I—I don't understand," the little man said. "How did I get here? My name is Morrison—Sylvester Morrison. I don't understand how I got here. I don't remember coming—"

"Morrison?" Sullivan blurted. "You're *Morrison?*"

McGee was feeling very sleepy. "That's right, Sully. He's Morrison. You better take him home and get him a doctor."

McGee heard astounded exclamations all around him, but he scarcely heard them. He had never felt sleepier in his life. But above the hubbub he heard Sullivan bellow:

"Gang of crooks besieging Headquarters! I thought they were cleaning up crime in this town!"

"Gosh, Sully—you can't believe—what you read in the papers," McGee said. And as he said it he slipped sidewards in his chair, unconscious.

McGee sat up in a comfortable bed and sipped soup. After two weeks of supervised mending, he was eager to be up; but they wouldn't let him get up for a while yet. He had to stay in bed and listen to visitors talk, especially Detective Sergeant James Baxter.

Baxter had just come in with a letter in his hands. McGee had laid it aside, but now, the soup-bowl drained, he took it up.

"Morrison went back to work today, Show-Me. He's all right again. I guess that girl and the young fellow're going to get married soon, too."

"They always do," McGee said, ripping open the envelope.

"It's funny how you cleared it up, Show-Me," Baxter

mused on. "Here I thought it was all proved that Leach killed Townland and then Townland killed Leach, and all the time—what's that? A check?"

McGee was blinking at the letter. It was signed by Spencer Kilgore, and it said something about deeply appreciating McGee's services. But Baxter could see only the check.

"Ten thousand bucks, Show-Me. Ten thousand bucks!"

"Box-Car," McGee said, "there's something I *want* to believe!"